HARRY MAZER is an acclaimed author
with numerous novels to his credit, includ-
ing *Snow Bound, Who Is Eddie Leonard?* (an
ALA Best Book for Young Adults), *The
Island Keeper*, and *Someone's Mother Is
Missing*. He and his wife, novelist Norma
Fox Mazer, are the authors of *The Solid
Gold Kid* (an ALA Best Book for Young
Adults and an IRA-CBC Children's
Choice) and *Bright Days, Stupid Nights*.
Harry Mazer is also the editor of the short
story anthology *Twelve Shots* (an ALA
Quick Pick), for which he wrote the story
"Until the Day He Died."

The Mazers have four grown children
and divide their time between Jamesville,
New York, and New York City.

D0981021

THE LAST
MISSION

Harry Mazer

LAUREL-LEAF
BOOKS

Published by
Dell Laurel-Leaf
an imprint of
Random House Children's Books
a division of Random House, Inc.
1540 Broadway
New York, New York 10036

"There's a Star Spangled Banner Waving Somewhere," words and music by Paul Roberts and Shelby Darnell: © Copyright 1942 by MCA MUSIC, A Division of MCA, Inc., New York, N.Y. Copyright Renewed. Used by permission. All rights reserved.

"Comin' In on a Wing and a Prayer," words and music by Harold Adamson/music by Jimmy McHugh, 1943. Used by permission.

Visit us on the Web! www.randomhouse.com/teens

Educators and librarians, for a variety of teaching tools, visit us at www.randomhouse.com/teachers

---

ISBN: 0-440-94797-9

RL: 5.6

Reprinted by arrangement with Delacorte Press

Printed in the United States of America

February 1981

40

OPM

*For sharing their memories with me, I'd like to
thank these former Eighth Air Force flyers:
Bob Peel, Bob Welter,
Harry Grey, and Bill O'Malley*

To the men I flew with in the 398th Bomb Group
of the Eighth Air Force during World War II,
and to my crew, Godfathers, Inc.

For the living: John F. Schmid,
William D. O'Malley, Jr., and Harry Grey.
And in memory of those who didn't return:

PILOT	*Second Lt. Allan H. Ferguson, Jr.*
COPILOT	*F/O John R. Halbert*
NAVIGATOR	*Second Lt. Howard U. Feldman*
ENGINEER	*Tech. Sgt. Joseph A. Heustess*
TAIL GUNNER	*Staff Sgt. Byron O. Young*
RADIO OPERATOR	*Tech. Sgt. Michael J. Brennan, Jr.*

PART I

THE CREW

"There's a Star Spangled Banner Waving Somewhere"
(Words and Music by Paul Roberts and Shelley Darnell, Leeds Music Corp., 1942.)

There's a Star Spangled Banner waving
  somewhere
In a distant land so many miles away
Only Uncle Sam's great heroes get to go there
Where I wish that I could also live some day
I'd see Lincoln, Custer, Washington, and Perry
And Nathan Hale and Colin Kelly, too!
There's a Star Spangled Banner waving
  somewhere
Waving o'er the land of heroes brave and true

If I do some great deed I will be a hero
And a hero brave is what I want to be
There's a Star Spangled Banner waving
  somewhere
In that Heaven there should be a place for me.

1

(October 1944. Alexandria Army Air Field, Louisiana.)

Jack Raab knelt in the shadow of the big bomber. It was early, but hot, and there was no shade anywhere on the airfield except under the wings of the plane. The six crewmen sprawled out under the B-17 were waiting for their officers. They were here for the last phase of training before going into combat. To Jack, the other enlisted men were everything he wasn't—older, tougher, self-confident. None of them seemed nervous.

Jack rapped his feet together, pleased with his boots' soft dark shine. *You're in the Army now*, the boots said to him, and it came over him like a shock, the way it did each time. Fifteen years old, and in the United States Air Corps.

Jack pulled his coveralls away from his sweaty back. They'd been waiting for nearly an hour. He blinked against the gritty Louisiana wind and wiped the dust from his boots. Ankle-high, brown, laced-up, round-tipped GI boots. A solid size 12, double E. He moved his feet so the ox-blood polished surface caught the light. The night before he'd broken them in, GI'd them. Scrubbed them with a brush and a strong yellow soap, then let them dry to the shape of his feet, and finally polished them with ox-blood polish.

He had never really believed he would fool the Air Corps this long. The only reason he had was his size. He had always been big for his age. At fourteen he'd been taller than his older brother and nearly as tall as his father, who was just a hair under six feet. Jack had never been sick a day in his life, but his brother, Irv, had been sick a lot. Irv had been born with a rheumatic heart. Their mother was always after Irv to be careful. Not that she had anything to worry about: The only things Irv liked to do were read and argue.

Jack liked action. He was on the street all the time, playing games—stickball, handball, touch football, and war games. Ever since the war started Jack and his friends had been playing commando, dividing into two teams, the Nazis and the commandos. Jack was always a commando, and when he got one of the "Nazis" he really knocked him around.

Jack had been ten in 1939 when the Germans occupied Poland. His parents and their friends had cried. Hitler's name was a curse. For years Jack's mother had sent presents and packages of clothes to their relatives in Poland—aunts, uncles, and a raft of cousins. Their pictures were in the family album

—poor people with wrinkled clothes, the women with scarves around their heads.

After the Germans marched into Poland, his mother's letters and packages all came back marked *Addressee unknown. Moved. No Forwarding Address.* "Hitler's rounding up the Jews," Irv said. He was the oldest of the three of them, the expert on everything. "He's driving the Jews out of their homes."

"He calls us a sub-race," Marcia, the youngest, said. "He doesn't think we're human."

"I hate Hitler!" Jack clenched his fists. "I curse him." As long ago as that he'd started dreaming about fighting Hitler.

He had nightmares about the Nazis coming to get his family. He'd hear them in the hall outside their apartment, their black boots striking the floor like the clop of horses' hooves. He'd wake up in a sweat, his heart pounding, feeling as if he were suffocating. He could only stop the terror by imagining that he was ready for them.

He was waiting behind the door, feet spread wide, knees bent, arms apart like ice tongs. His hands had awful power. His fingers would snap Nazi necks like green beans. . . .

It was after the Army rejected Irv because of his rheumatic heart that Jack decided he was the Raab who had to go in and fight Hitler. One morning, after everyone had left the house, he took Irv's birth certificate out of the bureau drawer and went downtown on the subway, to Grand Central Palace. He put the birth certificate down in front of the recruiting officer.

"Irving Raab?" the officer said, studying the paper.

"Yes, sir." Jack stood tall and stifflegged, thinking it was good his father had taught him to say "sir" to his elders. "But everyone calls me Jack, sir." He smiled, but he was scared.

"All right, soldier, in that line for your physical."

Jack wasn't worried about the physical. He was in perfect health, his feet weren't flat, and he had 20-20 vision. He was only afraid that just by looking at him the doctor would know he was fifteen. But he passed every test that day, and the next day as well.

When his notice came, he got it from the mailbox before anyone saw it. On the day he left he packed a bag and put a letter in the mailbox for his mother. He told her not to worry, that he was going to be traveling out west, the way his father had when he was young.

Later, waiting in Penn Station with the other recruits, every one older than he, Jack knew he was going to do something great in the Air Corps. He didn't know what, but it was in him, an expanding feeling that made him throw back his shoulders and stand tall.

He had six weeks of basic training in Miami, a week sitting around in San Antonio while the Army decided what to do with him, then ten weeks in Nevada learning to be a gunner on a B-17. Now he was in Louisiana for eight weeks of intensive crew-training.

"Got a butt?" Chuckie O'Brien tapped Jack on the arm. His copper-colored hair was streaked black with sweat. Jack produced the pack of Camels he kept in his breast pocket, and they moved away from the plane to smoke.

Jack carried a pack of cigarettes with him at all

times. It made him feel older. Taking a smoke, even taking the cigarette out of the pack, was something he was careful to do exactly right. Clip a corner of the new pack so just one or two cigarettes popped up above the top. Strike the match, cup the flame neatly between his hands, bend, light, inhale.

He lit Chuckie's cigarette, then his own. He took a deep drag and let the smoke slowly out of his mouth. Smoking that way made him feel hard and tough. *Commander Raab took a slow drag on his cigarette. Raab's band of Jewish volunteers, mere boys, but all with hearts like lions, were deep in Nazi territory. Their mission: Destroy Hitler.*

"Think those officers will ever come?" Chuckie said, fanning his flaming face.

When Chuckie and Jack met in gunnery school near Las Vegas and found out they were both from The Bronx, New York, they had become friends. Chuckie was short, red, and freckled all over like an Irish Setter, while Jack was tall, blue eyed, dark haired, and high colored. Chuckie came from the west Bronx, Jack from the east Bronx. Chuckie's people had come here from Ireland, Jack's from Poland.

"I swiped my first cigarette from my old man when I was ten years old," Chuckie said. "If he knew, he'd have belted me good. But he never found out I was smoking till I was fifteen. He raised holy hell, but he couldn't stop me."

Jack nodded. He and Chuckie were alike in a lot of ways. "Nobody stops me when I make up my mind, either." He wished he could tell Chuckie how he'd gotten into the Army, and what his real age was. What if he just came out with it? *Hey, Chuckie, by the way, I'm fifteen years old. What do you think of that?*

It was tempting, but better not. Too dangerous. Even if Chuckie meant to keep his secret, he might let it slip by accident. If the Army found that he'd lied to them, they wouldn't just boot him out and send him back to his family. Maybe in the beginning, but not now, not after all the training they'd given him, and all the money Uncle Sam had spent on him. No, they'd throw him in jail and toss away the key.

A Jeep was approaching. "They're coming," Chuckie said.

"About time—" Jack started to say, but suddenly he couldn't speak. What if the officers took one look at him, and knew he was a fake?

The first officer, the shortest one, came out of the Jeep like a jack-in-the-box. Behind him was another officer built like a bear. The last one, wrinkled, rumpled, and squinting as if he'd just gotten out of bed, came around the back of the Jeep.

All the enlisted men were on their feet now, lined up in front of the plane, not exactly standing at attention, but not slouching, either.

"I'm your pilot, Gary Martin," the little whip of a guy said. "My copilot, Lieutenant Milt Held." The bear smiled. "Our navigator, Lieutenant Sam Seppetone." Lieutenant Seppetone raised his heavy lids. Lieutenant Martin looked from one enlisted man to the other, his eyes lingering for a moment on Jack.

Jack wiped his hands down the sides of his coveralls, reminding himself of other times he'd been scared and nothing had happened. The day he enlisted—that had been the scariest day of his life.

"This is going to be my first and last speech," Lieutenant Martin was saying. "We're a crew, at least we're going to be one before we're done. We're going to fly combat together. All of us are in the same boat. I know there aren't going to be any goof-offs on my crew. No screw-ups, no gold bricks. I don't have to be an iron pants. None of you has been dragged into this. We're all volunteers, and that means we're here because we want to be. The Air Force only takes the best." He stopped and looked at each man. "And we are going to do our best. We're going to get everything we can out of our training missions."

He counted off on his fingers. "Formation flying. Target practice. Practice bombing runs. Navigation practice. This is combat training. Everything is here, except the enemy. Every one of these training missions is vitally important. What you learn could mean the difference between life and death."

Jack felt as if Lieutenant Martin were talking directly to him. Okay, let's go! he thought. He'd forgotten his fear, he was all fired up. He couldn't wait to get up into the air and start training. He was going to know his job as waist gunner inside and out. More than that!

He'd take Lieutenant Martin's place if he had to. Every chance he got he'd stand behind Martin in the pilot's compartment and learn how to fly. Just in case they were ever hit in combat and both pilots were hurt, Jack would step in. They'd be flying on just one engine, but it wouldn't matter. He'd bring the big ship down to a safe landing.

We owe our lives to you, Jack Raab! Lieutenant Martin would insist the Air Corps make him a pilot.

The newspapers would write up the story of the untrained Jewish kid who, alone, brought a B-17 down to a safe landing and saved his entire crew.

"Any questions?" Lieutenant Martin said.

The Jewish Kid straightened up proudly. *No questions. All clear and ready to go, sir!*

Lieutenant Martin crushed his officer's cap back on his head. "You want to say anything, Milt? Sam? Anybody else?" He looked around. "Who's my waist gunner?"

Before he could stop himself, Jack raised his hand. Kid stuff. He had to watch that. "Waist gunner, Jack Raab, sir," he said, snapping to attention.

Lieutenant Martin looked him up and down. "You're a big one, Jack."

Jack started to laugh, then tightened his lips. He thought he laughed too much, something else he had to watch.

"Who's my tail gunner?" Paul Johnson, a sharp-faced kid from Saginaw, Michigan, clicked his heels together smartly. There was a little smile on his face. Jack was sure Johnson was mimicking him.

Chuckie was the radio operator. The nose gunner was Fred Pratt. Old Man Pratt looked older than anyone else on the crew.

Dave Gonzalez, the ball-turret gunner, was from San Antonio, Texas. The other southerner was Billy Eustice, the flight engineer.

"Okay, you guys, let's go," Lieutenant Martin said. "Eustice, go over the plane with me. I want to get out of here, pronto. Too damn hot to hang around."

Jack helped Dave Gonzalez pull the props through, then stood by with a fire extinguisher as each of the four engines was started. When the pilot gave the signal he ducked around the propellers, into the prop wash, to pull the chocks from the wheels.

In the plane he went forward to Chuckie's radio room for takeoff. The three rear gunners always came forward for takeoff to ease the weight on the tail. Lieutenant Martin took the plane up smooth as silk. Jack caught Chuckie's eye and made the V for victory sign. Lieutenant Martin was an ace pilot!

Once they were in the air he went back to the waist in the big middle section of the plane. Dave Gonzalez went down to the ball through the waist. Chuckie's radio room was directly forward of the waist, and if Jack squatted down he could see Paul Johnson all the way in the back kneeling behind his tail guns.

There was a big window on either side of the waist, and a .50 caliber machine gun on a swivel set squarely in the middle of each window. Jack's job was to operate both guns.

Jack plugged in the intercom and pushed the button. "Waist to pilot." He wanted to do everything right. "Waist to pilot, over."

Martin's voice, thin and reedy, filled his headphone. "Pilot to waist, what is it?"

"Waist gunner in position, sir."

"Everything all right?"

"Yes, sir."

Below, Jack could see the Gulf of Mexico, the bluest blue he'd ever seen. *He was at the controls of his P-51 Mustang barreling and diving and twisting down through the German squadrons, scattering them like sheep . . . he caught an ME 109 in his sight . . . fired . . . and blew it from the sky. . . .*

"Tail gunner to pilot." Paul Johnson came on

the intercom. "Target plane coming up at six o'clock low."

Jack gripped his gun handles. The small AT-6, trailing a long white target, slid up under their plane. Jack had the target in his sights. When the order to fire came, he was ready, thumbs on the trigger buttons. He pressed the buttons and the guns coughed. The whole plane shook as other guns got the target plane in their sights.

Jack sniffed the burnt firecracker smell, bullet casings flew, the heat of the hardworking guns filled the plane. He'd hit the target! He was sure of it. Exhilarated, he moved the gun smoothly left and right. Long after they'd flown by the target area, the Jewish Kid swung his gun back and forth, alertly searching the sky for enemy aircraft.

2

Jack was the first one up every morning. As soon as his feet hit the floor he wanted the rest of the crew to wake up and *move*. "Come on, Chuckie." Jack yanked the covers off his friend. "Are you dead or alive?"

Chuckie opened one eye. "Dead."

Jack tightened the sheet on his bunk, making it taut enough to bounce a quarter on, the way he'd been taught in basic. "Your brain rots if you sleep too long, O'Brien."

"Hey, Eager Beaver!" Johnson reared up from his bunk. "Will you button up!" Jack hated being called Eager Beaver, but he couldn't help being the first one up, the first one in line, the first to answer their instructors' questions.

Jack wanted to learn everything the instructors had to teach them. They were spending several hours in the classroom each day. The more he learned, the closer Jack felt to being ready for combat.

They were flying training missions every day over the Gulf, sometimes twice a day. There were navigational flights at night, and they bombed mock targets over the water. On the ground they had simulated air battles with enemy fighters, using a motion-picture screen and camera gun. The German ME 109's and FW 190's swept across the screen. Press a button and, instead of bullets flying, the camera whirred.

After these "battles" the films would be shown in one of the classrooms. The officers came to watch how the gunners had done. The first time the battle films were shown was misery for Jack. As the film came on the screen there was a lot of laughing and groaning. Jack nervously chewed his knuckles as he waited for his film to be shown. Chuckie had "hit" one of their own planes, and he wasn't the only one.

When Jack's film finally was shown, he sank down against Chuckie, his hand over his face. A lot of sky, total misses, a glimpse of the tail of one of the fighter planes he was supposed to be shooting, and then a long shot of the front end of a B-17. If that film had been bullets, Jack would have killed their own bombardier, their navigator, and both pilots.

"Oh, my God," he muttered. He glanced at Lieutenant Martin, then sank lower in his chair. "Oh, my God," he groaned miserably.

Chuckie patted him on the shoulder. "Take it easy, Jack, or you're not going to survive this."

Jack didn't know how to take it easy. He was in the Army to learn to fight. He couldn't be cool or casual like the other guys. He knew he smiled too much, laughed too loud, groaned as if he were dying. Even the way he felt about their plane was excessive. He just couldn't help himself.

He loved their B-17. He thought of her as a big, bright, broad-winged bird, crisp and neat with her long sleek body, high upswept tail, and all those guns and turrets. Thirteen .50 caliber machine guns covered every possible enemy approach. Their plane was proud, beautiful, powerful. Jack knew that nothing could ever touch her.

What he liked most about training was when they were in the air as a crew, flying in formation, everybody in his position. Then, peering out the waist window, looking for the "enemy," Jack could almost believe it was the real thing. Jack's goal was to go overseas and fight. What was the use of being in the Army if he was going to spend the whole time in the States?

They were doing a lot of formation flying, because that was the way they'd be flying in combat. Six planes to a squadron. Three squadrons stacked at different altitudes to a group.

Formation flying was hard on the pilots. They had to hold the plane steady through all the turbulence caused by the prop wash of the planes ahead. There was a constant jerking up and down. At night, when they only had the dim running lights at the tip of the wings to guide them, the entire crew was on alert to avoid a midair collision. But a collision happened anyway.

Jack was looking out the starboard waist window and saw the whole thing. It was one of those hot days with a lot of thermals and sudden down-drafts. Earlier their own plane had been caught in a downdraft. Everything that wasn't tied down, including Jack, went floating up to the roof of the plane. It was like

going over a huge bump in a road. You went *up,* and
then you went *down.*

Lieutenant Martin was able to bring their plane
under control. The B-17 flying just below their wing
position wasn't so lucky. It dropped and landed
right on top of the plane below it. At first Jack
almost laughed. One plane riding piggyback on
another! "Chuckie, get over here," he yelled, motion-
ing to Chuckie in the radio room.

The plane on top jerked and bounced, then swung
way up in the air, almost hitting another plane before
righting itself. Chuckie stood at Jack's shoulder,
watching. Then they saw the plane below. Jack caught
his breath. It was slashed halfway through the waist,
almost exactly where Jack stood in their own plane.

"Jesus!" Chuckie gripped Jack's shoulder.

The plane was wobbling, dropping down. A man
bailed out. "See that!" Jack exclaimed.

"Jesus!" Chuckie crossed himself.

Another man came out. They counted as the men
bailed out, and their chutes opened. Six, Jack counted.
Seven . . . eight . . . eight men, eight chutes. Where
was the ninth? Was that the waist gunner? Was he
dead?

"The pilot's still in there," Chuckie said. As they
watched they saw the plane head out over the water,
then the last man, the pilot, bailed out.

It was only after that that they finally received
some instruction on bailing out. Fifteen minutes of
instruction from an unsmiling instructor.

"You." The instructor pointed at Jack. "Come up
here." He fastened the chute harness over Jack's shoulders and around his legs. "This is how it's done, and
this is the most important thing I'm going to tell you.

Keep the harness straps tight at all times. When that chute snaps open, and you're jerked up, it's gonna feel like this." He yanked the harness up on Jack. It caught him painfully in the groin.

"Hey!" Tears came to his eyes it hurt so much.

"What are you doing to my buddy?" Chuckie said, only half joking.

"Just letting you guys know you don't want any slack down there," the instructor said, "because if there is, you're going to be singing soprano for the rest of your life."

Most of the instructors were vets who'd completed their missions in Europe and were back home teaching the new crews. They were tough. No sympathy. They treated the new crews as if they were a hopeless lot, too raw, too green to be worth anything.

In another class a scrawny guy with a bouncy Adam's apple gave them instructions on ditching over water. "I feel sorry for you men who can't swim."

"Another undertaker," Chuckie whispered.

There were rafts on the planes and inflatable yellow rubber vests, called Mae Wests, that they wore over their chute harnesses. Blown up the vests gave them a big busty Mae West look.

There was a lot of equipment they had to learn about. Heated electric suits that looked like long underwear for the cold at high altitudes. Bulky insulated sheepskin-lined boots, and oxygen tanks, and masks so they could breath when they were flying three, four, or five miles high.

There was more to learn than they had time for, and for most things, no time for practice. But Jack was confident that the Air Force thought of everything. They were taking good care of him. He wished his mother knew. Not a day passed without his thinking about his family. And some nights he lay awake, missing them so much he cried. His mother, his father, Irv, Marcia . . . what were they thinking? Did they miss him? It made Jack's throat hurt to think about his mother. But it was better now than when he'd first joined up. Those first weeks of basic in Miami Beach had been hell. Jack had been lonely and afraid every minute that the Army would catch on to him. He and another guy shared a room on the eighth floor of the Ambassador Hotel. Reveille was at five A.M. He'd tumble down the stairs double time (elevators were off limits to enlisted men). Outside he'd lie down in the road and sleep until he was ordered up for roll call. He was tired all the time, he'd never been so tired in his life, tired at night, and still tired in the morning.

After roll call, up the eight flights of stairs again to make his bed. Then down again, on the double—everything on the double—to march to breakfast.

"Fall in! Count off! By the numbers. One! Two! Right face, forward march. On the double, Hup, Hup, Hup!" The corporal stuck Jack in front of the platoon because he was so tall. "Hup, two, three, four, hup, two, three," the corporal shouted. Jack wasn't used to taking such short steps. "Raab, get in step. You cow-flop chaser, yeah, you, shitface! Right foot, first foot, can't you keep in step, you're throwing the whole fucking line out."

There were drills, calisthenics in the sand, obstacle courses, the Manual of Arms, classes in physics and navigation. Someone shouting at you every step. The Golden Rule of the Army: Keep your eyes open and your mouth shut.

There was training with the Springfield '03 rifle and the .30 caliber carbine. He was good with the guns. He got a sharpshooter medal and couldn't write home about it. He started letters to his family, but he had to stop himself. It was too dangerous. It was better if they thought he was in California, or Oregon, or Alaska, so far away they wouldn't try to find him. He got a good-conduct ribbon. Nobody to tell. He was so afraid he'd say or do something wrong that he hardly talked to anyone those first few weeks. But he was glad he was in the Air Corps, glad and proud. They sang as they marched. "Off we go into the wild blue yonder, flying high into the sun. . . ." The Air Force song brought tears to Jack's eyes. He'd dream about coming home a hero, covered with ribbons and decorations. Maybe limping from a wound in his leg, and with a black eye patch over one eye. Everyone would cry when they saw him, his mother, his brother and sister, his cousins and aunts and uncles, even his father would be crying. And Jack would just smile and say, *I had to enlist . . . I had to go and fight Hitler. . . .*

3

"Where'd you guys meet?" Dave Gonzalez said to Jack and Chuckie. "You know each other before you got in the Army? You're always together." The three of them were on the chow line.

"We met in San Antonio," Jack said. "Got to know each other in gunnery school after that."

"San Antonio's my hometown," Dave said. His brown face glistened with sweat. "My whole family lives there."

"That where all the cookies come from?" Jack said. Dave got food packages from home that he shared with them almost every week.

"San Antone is where I washed out of pilot's training," Dave said. "Right in my hometown. I cried like a baby, I wanted to be a pilot so bad."

Jack took his tray of food and sat down. He knew what it was to want something that bad. He would have cried too if the Air Force had turned him down. He wished he could tell them how it had really been for him—how scared he'd been because of his age and lying . . . how sure he'd been that he was going to fail . . . how he could hardly believe, even now, that he'd done it. It was something he kept wanting to talk about, and couldn't, not even to Chuckie.

In the barracks that night the guys started talking about Dave, who'd gone over to the PX for candy and cigarettes. Billy Eustice, Johnson, Chuckie, and Jack were playing poker.

"Dave's as black as some of our niggers back home," Billy said in his soft southern drawl.

The word nigger made Jack stiffen. Guys in the Army were always figuring out where everyone fit. Eustice and Johnson had tackled Jack right in the beginning. What kind of name was Raab? Where did he come from? What was his religion? As if just being himself wasn't enough.

"Gonzalez looks Spanish to me," Old Man Pratt said. He was playing solitaire on his foot locker. Pratt never gambled. He was careful with his money. He was the only married enlisted man, and his wife was expecting a baby any day.

"He could be Puerto Rican," Chuckie said. "Or Mexican."

Jack slapped down a card. "What difference does it make, O'Brien?" All this talk was getting on his nerves. Maybe he wasn't getting enough sleep. The night before he'd woken in a sweat because he'd dreamed the MP's were coming for him.

Eustice was still after Dave the next day. They were all waiting for the mail clerk to open the mail-room window. "Out of curiosity, Dave," Billy said, "we were talking last night. What are you, Spanish, or Mex?"

"Hey, Billy," Jack said, reddening, "don't start that again."

"I'm a hundred percent American," Dave said. "What are you?"

Billy smiled his soft embarrassed smile. "You know what I mean. What kind of American are you-all?"

"The same kind you-all are!"

"Billy doesn't mean anything bad," Chuckie said.

"Then let him keep his mouth shut," Dave said.

"Adams . . . Baker . . . Carlos. . . ." The mail clerk called the names alphabetically. "Dunlop . . . Fortunato . . . Gonzalez. . . ."

Dave received a couple of letters and a package and walked away.

The closer the mail clerk got to the R's the more tense and excited Jack became. He never skipped mail call even though he never received any mail. He went because he didn't want any questions asked, but also because he couldn't stop hoping. Everyone got mail. Why not him? He'd made up a whole story—his father was in Alaska building barracks for the Army, no brothers or sisters, and his mother was dead.

"You're almost an orphan," Chuckie had said. Chuckie had a younger brother, parents, and a girl-friend, Margie. They all wrote to him.

Chuckie received three letters. He waved them in the air, then ran off, tearing one open.

"Oblensky . . . Petroff . . . Pratt. . . ." Fred stepped forward. Wasn't he glad? Jack wondered. Not even a little smile out of old pokerface Pratt. Just put his mail in his pocket and sauntered off.

"Putter . . . Purcell. . . ." Jack's heart was pounding. He'd be the first R. Raab, then Race. *Come on, call Raab . . . Raab . . . Raab . . . Raab. . . .*

"Race," the mail clerk droned. "Raconi . . . Rammer . . . Root . . . Sands . . . Soboloff. . . ."

Nothing for Jack. He knew there wouldn't be. Nobody knew he was here, so how could anyone write to him? But he couldn't hold back a choking feeling of disappointment.

He had bought a writing kit in the PX for ninety-eight cents. Every guy on the crew had a writing kit, so he'd bought one, too. He also had a sewing kit to sew on his chevrons when he was promoted, and a shaving kit to shave with when he grew a beard.

Every day he fingered his jaw hopefully. Not a hair, not a bristle. "Smooth as a baby's ass," Johnson said, catching Jack at it. Jack used the shaving kit twice a week anyway. He'd heard that shaving helped your beard come in.

Jack wasn't the only beardless wonder. Billy Eustice didn't shave that much, either. Sometimes, though, Jack got discouraged. No beard, no mail. If he could just get a letter sometimes, even once a week—but to get a letter, he'd have to write a letter. Who could he write to?

One night, after chow, he perched on his foot-locker with his writing kit open on his lap. In the bunk next to his, Chuckie was sprawled out, writing page after page. "How do you find so much to write about?" Jack said. Chuckie looked up.

"Talent, Jack." He was in his green GI shorts, with his dog tags and Christopher medal on a chain around his neck.

Jack looked down at his blank paper. The only person he could think of to write was Dotty Landon, but he hardly knew her. "Dear Dotty, how are you? I am fine. Remember Miami Beach?" A great beginning,

but then he stopped. He traced over the letters of
Dotty's name. If he could just think of something to
say that didn't sound dumb and *young*. He chewed on
the end of his pencil.

Did Dotty even remember him? He'd only met her
a couple of times. But he remembered her! Long pale
legs, dark hair cut straight across her forehead in
bangs. Pretty, nice, really friendly!

He'd met her at the very end of basic training. He'd
gone down to the shore to walk on the sand, and he
noticed a girl wading into the ocean.

"Hey!" he yelled. "Stop! There are jellyfish out
there."

He ran to the edge of the water and explained about
the guy in his squadron who'd gotten stung by a jellyfish and how his leg had blown up like a balloon.

"Jellyfish?" she said. The waves curled over her
bare feet. "Sure you don't mean jamfish?"

"Either way," he said. "You ever been in Miami
before?" Her skin was pale.

"First time."

"I bet you're from New York," he said.

"How'd you know?" She pulled on her sandals.
"How come you know so much?"

It turned out she was from Brooklyn, vacationing
with her mother. And since he was from The Bronx,
it was as if they were from the same country. They
walked along the sand, comparing Miami to New
York City. New York City, they agreed, was much
better, even if it was dirtier and more crowded. It
was the easiest time Jack ever had talking to a girl.

Of course Dotty's thinking he was eighteen helped.
And so did his being in uniform. Girls were always

looking at him now. The uniform made a difference. The girls he passed on Collins Avenue smiled at him. A couple of times girls tried to get him to talk, but he was still too shy. Once a gang of girls went by and whistled. His face turned red. Girls had never noticed him that much before. He liked it. He began dreaming about having a girlfriend of his own, but he didn't really think it would happen. Then he met Dotty.

They met a couple of times and went bike riding. When they parted, Dotty wrote her name and address on a slip of paper. Jack put it in his wallet. "I'll write you, Jack," Dotty said, "but you'll have to write first, and let me know where they've assigned you."

Since then Jack had thought a lot about Dotty. He had imagined writing to her, but he had never actually done it. Too nervous, too shy. What would he say? What if she didn't remember him? In his head he'd write up a storm, but when it came to really doing it—nothing!

"Dear Dotty . . ." He looked over the nine words he'd written so far. They were so ordinary. *How are you? I am fine.* He sounded about ten years old!

Dear Dotty, This is Jack Raab, the guy you met on the beach in Miami. The tall guy in the Air Corps. I'm an aerial gunner now on a B-17, the best bomber the USAAC has. We'll be going overseas pretty soon. We're training hard. Can't tell you any more without being censored, but I sure wish you would write back to me. It's pretty lonely not getting any mail from anybody. . . .

He chewed on his pencil. Dotty was eighteen years old. She probably had lots of boyfriends. Even if he finished a letter and sent it, he could just imagine her getting it. *Jack Raab? Jack Raab? Who's he?* And then she'd throw the letter away.

He never finished the letter. Instead he began studying the little calendar in his writing kit. October was gone. November was half over, and all they were doing was practicing. Practicing, practicing, and more practicing. It was enough! Jack wanted to get going. *Overseas. Combat.*

He was still thinking about it the next morning. He pushed the breakfast tray away. Chipped beef in a cream sauce on toast. "Shit on a shingle again!" It turned Jack's stomach.

"Eat it," Chuckie said. "It's good for you."

"You want it? You can have it." He reached into his pocket for a cigarette.

Chuckie glanced at him. "Cut out the cigarettes before breakfast, Jack. No wonder you're so fucking jumpy."

"Fuck off," Jack answered automatically. The swearing in the Army was like nothing he'd ever heard before. When he was home, he'd known all the swear words and used them sometimes, but never where his mother or any grown-up could hear. But in the Army everyone swore, all the time, everywhere, about everything.

At first it had made Jack uncomfortable, and then he started swearing like everyone else. He hardly noticed it anymore.

He looked around the chow hall. Jack could pick the vets right out by their leather jackets and the way they wore their hats crushed back on their heads. Jack had done the same thing to his cap. Pulled out the stiffener, wrung the hat out in the shower, and twisted it out of shape. Those crushed caps were the devil-may-care badges of the seasoned flying crews. But, somehow, Jack's cap never looked the same on him as it did on the veterans. Those were the guys who had flown twenty-five, thirty, or more missions, and come home. They were real heroes.

Jack drummed his fingers on the table.

"What are we doing all this practicing for?" Jack said to Chuckie. "I want to get over there. I want to fight! What's all this practicing about? Let's go! Let's get those Nazis!"

"When the Führer says," Chuckie sang, keeping time with his fork, "we are the master race, we heil—splaaat!"—he gave the Bronx raspberry—"right in the Führer's face! Not to love the Führer is a great disgrace! So, we heil—splaaat!—heil—right in the Führer's face!"

He shook Jack. "Cheer up, buddy, we're getting them. We're pushing them back. What difference does it make if it's us or some other guys?"

Jack knew it didn't matter who got Hitler. But, still, he wanted to be the one.

"There's Higbee," Chuckie said. They watched as the sergeant carried his tray to a table right across from them.

"The master sergeant told me he flew a double tour," Jack said in an awed voice. "Fifty combat missions with the Eighth."

Sergeant Higbee wore silver gunner's wings on his chest, and underneath a Purple Heart with an Oak Leaf Cluster which meant he got hit twice. "He's got so many Oak Leaf Clusters on his Air Medal," Jack said, "you can't even count them."

"I heard he got the Distinguished Flying Cross for

shooting down three German fighter planes," Chuckie
said. They watched Higbee pass. He walked with a
stiff gait. He was teaching gunnery classes now on the
base. He was all done with combat.

Higbee was done, Jack thought, now it was Raab's
turn. *Alone with his gun, a fighter pilot in his own
plane . . . tracking the black German fighters. . . .
Three came whipping past the nose at twelve o'clock
low. . . . Raab blasted away, there was a trail of black
smoke. . . . One down . . . then another . . . and a
third. Congratulations, Sergeant Raab, three more
Nazi kills to your credit. I will recommend you for the
DFC. . . .*

Jack never spoke to Sergeant Higbee—he wouldn't
have had the nerve. But whenever he saw him around
the base he followed him with his eyes. Followed that
worn leather flight jacket with the name of Higbee's
plane stenciled in red on the back. SATAN'S WAGON.
And underneath fifty little gold bombs, one for each
mission.

The day the new sergeant ratings were posted outside the orderly room, Chuckie and Jack went running.

Jack's eyes swept down the long row of typewritten
names. Eustice . . . Gonzalez . . . Johnson . . .
O'Brien. . . .

Everyone on his crew had made it. Where was his
name? He began to feel sick. He'd been passed over!
He'd have to stay back when the rest of the crew went
overseas.

"We made it, buddy." Chuckie was hanging on
Jack. Jack's eyes focused, and he saw his name. Sergeant Jack Raab. Six months ago he'd been a fresh-

man at Christopher Columbus High School, and now he was a sergeant in the United States Air Force. Oh, how he wished his father could see him now! Grinning, he pushed Chuckie away and snapped to attention.

"Sergeant Raab requesting an overnight pass."

"Sergeant O'Brien turning you down."

"Try it, Sergeant O'Brien! You don't outrank me."

"Your face is dirty, Sergeant Raab. Get out of here before I throw you in the stockade."

That night he took out his sewing kit and sewed the sergeant's patch on his cotton and olive-drab shirts, and on his garrison jacket.

The promotion made him believe that he was going to get into the war soon. Any day now—well, in another three or four weeks—they'd be receiving their shipping orders. They'd be going overseas. Leaving the country. Jack had never really thought about it that way till right now. It had just been an intense wish. Now it was going to come true. It made him feel excited, and a little scared. He'd be leaving the United States, leaving his family behind, going farther away than he'd ever gone in his life.

But going into combat was a bigger divide than the Atlantic Ocean. It was the test. It was what all his training had been about. And though Jack had dreamed over and over about all the great things he'd do in combat, deep down inside himself he didn't know how he'd really act until the time came.

4

Two weeks after the sergeant ratings were posted, they completed their training. While they waited for their orders the whole crew got a weekend pass to New Orleans. All the enlisted men went except Old Man Pratt. He didn't want to leave the base in case his wife had the baby.

"Afraid to part with a buck," Johnson said. He knotted his tie into a big Windsor knot. "Right, Pratt?"

"Right." Pratt was unperturbed. "I'm staying close to the phone. I've got a feeling that Evie's going to call with good news."

"Don't forget the cigars," Dave Gonzalez said.

"Cigars," Johnson said. "This guy'll hand out cigarette butts."

Jack was dressed and ready to go long before Chuckie. "Come on, Chuckie, what's taking you so long?" Jack was eager to get off the base. Almost two months since he'd been anywhere. And with his brand new sergeant stripes on his sleeve, he was dreaming about the admiring looks he was going to get.

Chuckie poured Aqua Velva over his cheeks, and rubbed Vitalis into his hair. He put on a starched OD shirt he'd had tailored so it fit him snugly. "I gotta make myself pretty for the girls," he said, buttoning up his shirt. "Those girls in the French Quarter are lined up waiting for me."

"How about Margie?" Jack said as they walked to the bus. "I thought she was the only one."

"She is, Jack. I'm just going to have a little fun. Nothing serious."

On the bus they were all jammed together and singing to pass the time. "We're a sharp-looking crew," Jack said. Their pants and shirts were creased and ironed, their boots and brass were shining.

"But wait till you see us tomorrow," Johnson added.

In New Orleans they headed straight for the French Quarter. Dave Gonzalez and Paul Johnson went off to Bourbon Street to hear some Dixieland. Then Chuckie spotted a couple of girls. He and Billy went after them. Jack tagged after. Chuckie swung in on one side of the girls, and Billy on the other. Jack started to follow, then stopped. What was he going for? He didn't know anything about girls. He didn't know how to flirt. He'd never even kissed a girl. He let Chuckie and Billy get farther and farther away, and then they went around the corner, and he was alone. For a while it was fun going down one crowded street after another. He held himself tall and straight, hoping a girl would notice him and smile. At times he let his cheek twitch, and limped as if he had a war wound.

The French Quarter with its narrow streets and crowded buildings reminded him a lot of Greenwich Village in New York. The people even talked like New Yorkers, not like southerners. He stopped to look at a building covered with fancy metal grillwork that looked just like climbing English ivy.

After the war he'd become an architect . . . his office would be on top of the Empire State Building . . . he'd put up a building taller than the Empire State Building . . . a mile in the air . . . the tallest building in the world. The Raab building. Nobody would ever have seen anything like it. In the newspapers they'd write,

**War Hero and Flying Ace, Jack Raab,
Designs Another Unbelievably Daring
Building. . . .**

In a store window he caught a glimpse of himself—the glitter of his gunner's wings, overseas cap set at a jaunty angle on his head. *The tall handsome combat veteran was modest about his achievements . . . girls followed him everywhere . . . he preferred to be alone. . . .*

He kept walking. GI's everywhere. More GI's than civilians. Jack was getting hungry and tired. He looked into one restaurant after another. They all seemed too fancy, or too busy. He kept moving. It wasn't so much fun anymore.

What was the big deal about coming to New Orleans? Just a lot of narrow dirty streets. He felt worse and worse. He was in a strange place surrounded by strangers. Nobody knew him, and nobody cared. Everyone was with someone. But Jack, for all his posturing and posing, could have been invisible. Nobody noticed him.

He went into a movie house. It was a place to go where he didn't have to act or make believe. He slid into a seat. The theater was full of soldiers. The movie was *North Star* with Anne Baxter and Farley Granger. Anne and Farley were Russians. He was a soldier, and she was a brave partisan fighter. For a little while Jack forgot everything while Anne and Farley fought the Nazis.

When he came out it was nighttime. For a minute he didn't know where he was. Part of him was still in Russia, fighting side by side with Farley and Anne, and part of him was back home in The Bronx, coming out of the Allerton Theatre. Out of the corner of his eye he saw a man in a short wool jacket standing in front of a luncheonette window. There was a newspaper folded in his hip pocket.

"Dad!" Jack said. The man looked around. A stranger, of course. Jack turned away, and then, like a black ocean wave, homesickness caught him. Tears came to his eyes.

What was he doing here? He hated this place. He should never have left the base. He started to run, not looking at anyone, ducking and dodging around people. He wouldn't stay overnight in New Orleans. What for?

He didn't stop running until he got to the bus station. There were posters on every wall. "Use it up, wear it out, make it do, or do without." "Shhh! The enemy is listening!" This, under a picture of Uncle Sam with his finger to his lips. Another showed Uncle Sam pointing sternly, saying "Uncle Sam Wants YOU! Enlist NOW."

Jack took out his wallet to find his return ticket, and saw the slip of paper with Dotty's address and phone number. He badly wanted someone to talk to. He couldn't call home. He didn't trust himself not to give everything away. He knew that if he heard his mother's voice, he'd break down.

He went to one of the phones on the wall and without giving himself time to think he gave the operator Dotty's number in Brooklyn.

The phone rang. He wondered if her phone was in the lobby the way it was in his building at home. "Hello?" someone said.

"Hello," Jack said. "D—"

"One moment, please," the operator interrupted. She told Jack to deposit his money. Each time a quarter dropped into the machine, it was like an explosion in his stomach. Now he was scared. What had he done?

"Go ahead," the operator said.

"Can I speak to Dorothy Landon?"

"Speaking. Is that you, Teddy?"

"Hello," he stammered. He could feel the hair lifting from his scalp.

"Teddy?" she said again.

He was struck dumb. What was he going to say?

"Teddy!" she exclaimed. "Is that you, or isn't it? Where are you calling from, Teddy?"

"No, it's Jack," he got out. "Jack Raab."

"Who?" she said.

She didn't remember. He felt damp and itchy in his wool OD's. Hang up, he told himself. This is going to be bad. "I met you in Miami Beach . . . four months ago. July. The jellyfish. Remember the jellyfish?"

"The jelly—oh! Oh, yes. Yes," she spoke slowly. "I remember now," she said. He'd forgotten how slowly she spoke. How could he remember? He'd only seen her twice.

"Remember we met on Collins Avenue just before I left," he said. "We went bike riding."

"Oh, yes, yes, I remember."

He didn't believe her. He clutched the receiver. "I'm calling from New Orleans," he said.

"What? I'm sorry, I can't hear you."

"New Orleans. Louisiana!" he said loudly.

"You're calling all that way? You're spending a lot of money."

"Well, I'm a sergeant now. I get plenty of money."

"What? This connection—I didn't hear you. What'd you say?"

"I said, it doesn't matter."

"Oh."

Silence hummed over the wire. He was dripping with sweat.

"Hello," she said. "Are you still there?"

"Still there."

"What's your weather like there?" she said in her slow way. "It's cold and damp here." Then, suddenly, "I didn't forget you, Jack. I just—when you called, I was so surprised. It's been a long time. I thought you forgot."

"No, I thought you did."

"No, Jack. I remember how you warned me about the jellyfish."

"Jamfish," he said.

She laughed. "Yes, I remember all that. When we went bike riding we stopped for coconut drinks."

"That's right," he said. He felt a little better. "I started a letter, but. . . . They keep us busy, they keep us hopping, so I—"

"Jack Rabbit," she said. "Terrible pun! Sorry!"

"No, that's funny," he said.

"Oh, you're too nice!" There was another little silence. Then she said, "I just got home from the Hunter library. The phone was ringing when I walked in the apartment."

"Hunter College?" he said.

"Yes. I feel awful when I think of what other people are doing for the war effort. So many terrible things happening in the world . . . but I just don't see where I fit in. Listen, Jack, this is going to cost you so much money—"

"No—" He waved his hand grandly. "What's money?"

"It's cheaper to write."

"I'm not such a good letter writer," he said.

"Oh, I bet you're better than you realize," Dotty said. "Jack, can you give me your address? I'll write you. But if you get a letter from me, you have to answer."

"I will," he said fervently. "I promise. I'll write you. I really will." He gave her his address. "When we go overseas it'll be different," he said.

"I know," she said. "It'll be an APO, and we'll write on V-Mail. I have two uncles overseas, Jack. When will you be going?"

"Soon," he said. It made him feel good, steady and strong, to say that. Had Teddy been overseas? "Who's Teddy?" he said. "Is he in the service?"

"Teddy?" She laughed. "He's my little cousin. He's

still in high school. They live upstate and he calls me all the time. Jack, you better hang up, or you won't have any money left to buy stamps. Good-bye, Jack."

"I'll come see you on my furlough," he said. "Good-bye, Dotty." But he didn't hang up. He didn't want to break the connection. "I don't think I'll hang up, Dotty," he said.

"Then we'll just have to go on talking."

"I don't mind," he said.

"But maybe we'll run out of things to say, Jack! And we'll just be breathing long distance, a dollar a breath."

"That's okay," he said, liking her more and more. "Money doesn't mean anything to me. People are more important than money."

"That's sweet, Jack, but I'll feel guilty if we don't hang up. On the count of three—are you ready?"

"No," he said.

"Well, get ready. Jack, don't forget what you promised. You're going to answer my letter."

"I won't forget!"

"How many other girls have you promised to write, Jack?"

"You're the only one!"

"Wish I could believe that. One—"

"You can believe me, Dotty."

"Okay, Jack. Two—"

"Dotty—"

"*Three*. Bye-bye, Jack." She hung up.

That night, after Jack returned to the base and sacked out, he lay awake, thinking about Dotty. Going over the phone call in fifteen different ways and still not believing that he'd done it, and that she'd been so wonderful. He wanted to remember all the things she'd said, the sound of her laugh, the slow way she talked, and how she'd teased him.

He'd go see her on his furlough. Maybe even double date with Chuckie and Margie. But even better than that would be visiting her when he came back after he'd completed his missions. Because then he'd be wearing his uniform with all his ribbons and medals. One of his ribbons would be a Purple Heart. His sleeve would be pinned up.

"Hello, sweetheart," he'd say through his front teeth, like Humphrey Bogart. "Don't look so sad, sweetheart. I just caught a hunk of flak in my arm. No harm done."

Two weeks later they were told to report to the orderly room for their shipping orders. Fred Pratt was at the PX. He'd been called to the phone about half an hour before. "Come on, what are we waiting for?" Johnson said. "Let's go. Fred can follow us."

"No, let's wait for him," Jack said. "Let's go as a crew."

Billy looked at his wristwatch. "We'll give him ten more minutes," he said in his soft voice. "Okay, you-all?"

Before the ten minutes were up, Old Man Pratt arrived, poker faced as usual. "Where you been?" Dave said. "We're waiting for you. We're getting our shipping orders."

Pratt didn't say anything, just pulled a box of cigars from under his arm and opened it. Every cigar had a pink band. "Have a cigarette butt," he said, offering it first to Johnson. "Have two."

Everyone crowded in, pounding him on the back and congratulating him. "Her name is Patricia," Fred said. "Patricia Jean Pratt. And all you guys are going to be her godfathers."

"This is the first time I ever saw Pratt smile," Chuckie said to Jack, a few minutes later, as they walked over to the orderly room.

It was funny how Fred's becoming a father made him seem even older to Jack. Like an older brother. Jack had felt close to all the guys, not just Chuckie. Pratt was steady, you could always depend on him. Dave was moody, went down in the dumps, but came up fast. Johnson still bothered Jack with his sharp tongue. Jack was careful around him. Billy, on the other hand, was like a marshmallow, not a sharp spot anywhere. Even his prejudice wasn't sharp. He hung around more with Dave than with anyone else.

Their shipping orders were for Lincoln, Nebraska, where they'd pick up a brand-new B-17 to fly overseas. They were given ten days to get to Lincoln. Enough time for all of them to get home, though not for long. But everyone was going. Jack, too, back to New York City. He couldn't hang around the base alone. There would be too many questions raised. Why wasn't he going home like the others? So, where else could he go but to New York?

He couldn't see his family, but Dotty was there. She had been as good as her word and written him. He'd read and reread her letter. "Dear Jack, I hope you don't think I forgot you. After Miami I kept waiting for your letter, and when it didn't come I said, *the skunk forgot me!* I'm awfully glad you called. You can see from the date I sat right down to write you. *RSVP!* And when you come to New York, I hope you'll call me, *at least!*"

The day after they received their shipping orders,

the whole crew had its official Air Corps crew picture taken. They lined up in front of a B-17 with one of the three-bladed props behind them. The officers knelt in front, and the enlisted men stood in back.

Sergeant Billy Eustice was at one end of the line with his overseas cap pulled squarely down over his round smiling face. Next to him, Sergeant Chuckie O'Brien with his jaunty Irish grin, and then Sergeant Fred Pratt looking straight into the camera. As usual, Sergeant Gonzalez looked a little worried, and as usual Sergeant Johnson looked a little bored. And finally, there was Sergeant Jack Raab of the United States Air Corps, looking off into the wild blue yonder.

5

Jack and Chuckie left on furlough together. They hopped a C-47 cargo plane to Kansas City. In Tulsa, however, Jack was bumped by a brigadier general. Chuckie offered to wait with him for the next plane, but Jack refused.

"Go home. See your family, see Margie. I'll call you."

"Got my number?"

Jack patted his wallet. "Right here." He had Dotty's letter, too, and her address and phone number. He had decided if he could get up the nerve he'd call her for sure. Chuckie was talking about him and Margie going out with Jack and Dotty.

After Chuckie's plane left, Jack checked the long list of GI's waiting for rides, and decided to take his chances on the road. He wasn't in that much of a rush to get to New York. Even if he could see Dotty, what was he going to do rest of the time? He couldn't see his family. He couldn't even call them.

A ground-crew chief drove him in his Jeep to the gate. Jack stood at the side of the road, B-4 bag at his feet, thumb in the air. There was a bunch of guys hitching at the gate. A salesman driving a big black thirty-eight Buick picked up four of them, including Jack.

"I never pass up a hitchhiking soldier," he said.

Jack sat in back, dozing, looking at the country-side. Toward evening he stared at lighted windows of passing houses. Sometimes, someone was at the window . . . a woman . . . or a child looking out.

Right now his father would be washing up after work. Then he'd pull up a chair to the radio and listen to the news. The radio, a mahogany cabinet with sliding doors and brass dials, was their one good piece of furniture. The top was covered with silver-framed pictures of their family. A big one of his parents on their wedding day, his mother in a white satin wedding dress, his father looking years younger in a black tux and boiled shirt-front. There were smaller pictures of him and Irv in shorts and sleeveless Camp Owoqua shirts, and of his sister, Marcia, chin up like a movie star, showing her distinguished Raab profile. Everyone said that Marcia resembled Gene Tierney, the movie star, and Marcia believed it.

Could he call home without giving anything away? "Mom, it's me, Jack. How are you?" She wouldn't have to know where he was, or what he was doing. But she was sharp. From any little hint she'd guess the truth. No, he couldn't call. He'd just see Dotty, and pretend his family wasn't even there.

He told himself soldiers didn't have an easy life. He remembered the stories his grandmother used to tell him about her brother Joseph. He was taken into

the czar's army when he was eleven years old and
never came back. "The czar, may he perish from this
earth," his grandmother would say, even though the
czar had been dead for over twenty years.

The salesman dropped Jack in St. Louis. The others
were going on with him to Chicago. "Thanks a million," Jack said.

"Good luck, soldier. Keep your pecker up and your
head down."

Jack stood by the side of the road again. He'd
hardly dropped his B-4 bag when a truck driver carrying cow hides to New York City stopped for him.

The truck driver, Kenny, had a brother in the in-
fantry. "Soldier, this war is crazy. What's it doing for
us?"

"What about Hitler?" Jack said.

"What about him?" The truck driver looked at
Jack.

Something hot and urgent gathered in Jack. "I'm
a Jew," he said.

"No offense," Kenny said quickly. "I don't like
Hitler either."

It was morning when they made Indianapolis. In
a dirty little men's room in a roadside diner, Jack
brushed his teeth. He and Kenny ate eggs and drank
coffee, then started off again.

They rode through Muncie, Decatur, and Lima.
Rain smeared the windows. Jack had been on the road
for twenty-four hours. He was dazed. He slept all the
way through Pennsylvania and Jersey. Kenny dropped
him off in Manhattan near the Holland Tunnel. It
was three days since Jack had left the base. He and
Kenny shook hands.

Jack walked to the BMT line. He felt tired and

excited. His face was flushed. New York—the buildings, the noise, the crowds. Just being here excited him. This was home, and everywhere he looked he saw people he thought he recognized. He decided not to go to The Bronx. Too close to home, too tempting. Better to go to Brooklyn where Dotty lived.

He took the Coney Island Express to Brooklyn. It was the middle of the afternoon, and the car was half empty. Jack rocked back and forth with the swaying motion. When the doors opened at Sea Gate station there was a blast of cold wintry air, and the smell of the sea. Jack shouldered his bag. Dotty lived somewhere close by, but he was too tired to think about her.

He found a room in a house that had a yellow silk panel hanging in the window. There was a blue star on the yellow panel. It meant they had someone in the service. Next to it was a hand lettered sign: ROOM TO RENT. A stocky woman with streaks of gray in her hair opened the door. She had a kind face with dark circles under her eyes. She looked Jack over, then invited him in.

"We have someone in the service, too, sergeant," she said as he followed her up the stairs.

"Yes, m'am." He was tired, so tired, too tired to talk.

"It's my daughter's room. She's in the WAVES. We're always glad to rent it to a soldier."

A maple bed, a maple desk, a maple bureau covered with a clean white cloth. High-school banners on the wall. The moment Mrs. Esposito left the room Jack fell down on the bed, reached for the quilt, and was asleep.

He woke up groggy. It was morning. He washed

and changed his clothes, then went downstairs. "There you are," Mrs. Esposito said. "Come in, and sit down. I'll have breakfast for you." She fed him eggs, sausage, and stacks of toast with orange marmalade.

"This is great," Jack kept saying. "This is great. Thanks, really."

She glanced at the Mogen David that was hanging outside his shirt. "You're a Jewish boy?"

"Right," Jack said. "I'm Jewish."

"I thought so right away when I saw you," she said. "I don't take everyone who knocks on my door. But I liked the way you looked."

He sat and talked to Mrs. Esposito for a long time. She was friendly. It felt good to be in a real house again. She showed him pictures of her daughter Clara in a big white satin-covered album.

Later he took a long walk along the boardwalk. It was cold, sunny, and windy. His head cleared, but he was still tired. Mothers with babies bundled up in carriages glanced at Jack as they passed. There were old couples sitting in the sun. He walked with one hand on his cap to keep it from blowing off. He thought about Dotty, but he didn't go anywhere near her street. Dotty . . . Dotty. . . . He said her name, but it was unreal. He was scared to see her.

He ate hamburgers in a White Tower. Maybe Dotty would walk in. He'd give her his lopsided Jimmy Stewart smile. What if he recognized her, and she didn't know him? He ate more hamburgers and french fries. He was hungry, he couldn't seem to fill up.

He walked along the street. He kept seeing people who reminded him of his parents. Every woman at a distance was his mother, and every man, his father. He began to think he'd actually run into his mother.

What would he say? "Hi, Ma!" What would he do?

If only he could see them, just for a little while. Maybe he could go see his grandmother. She was in her eighties, she might not recognize the uniform. No, she would. She was old, but she was smart. What had his mother told her to explain his not visiting anymore? It hurt to think about his grandmother, it hurt to think about his family. He had never thought it would be this bad.

Then he got the idea that he'd buy some civilian clothes and go see his family. They wouldn't know he was in the service if he didn't wear his uniform. He'd just show up for a few days, and then disappear again. But first he'd call them.

Twice he went by phone booths and thought of calling home. He'd talk to his mother, tell her he was working for a long-distance trucker. But he didn't trust himself. If he heard his mother's voice he'd start crying, and then he'd tell her everything. It would be the dumbest thing in the world. He was so close to going overseas. He couldn't risk giving that up.

He went into a candy store to buy a chocolate bar. He was feeling sad. He wanted to eat something sweet. There was a phone booth in the back. *Call,* he thought, *they can't see you over the phone. What are you afraid of? You'll just talk to them and see how it goes. Maybe you won't see them, maybe you will.*

He ran from the candy store, he was so afraid of what he'd do. He didn't try again. He walked around for a long time, just moving, just putting one foot in front of the other.

When he got back to the Espositos', Jack went to bed early. Birds were singing when he woke up. He thought he was home. "Mom?" he called. For a moment he was sure he was home. Then he remembered where he was.

Later he went out again. He called Chuckie's home, but nobody answered. In front of a newsstand he met a merchant seaman. They started talking, then went into a bar for a beer.

The seaman, Oscar Freed, peered at Jack. He wore thick glasses. "I couldn't get in the service with these eyes. I'm on a freighter, it's like a shooting gallery, and we're the pigeons. We've been sailing in the North Atlantic, back and forth to Murmansk with supplies for the Russians. You get torpedoed in those waters and you freeze in thirty seconds."

Jack took a long swallow of beer. He started to tell Oscar about the plane he'd seen nearly cut in half, but Oscar interrupted. "You know where you guys would be without the Merchant Marines? Who do you think brings all the war supplies to Europe? The oil and the guns? And the ammo? There wouldn't even be a war without the Merchant Marines."

Oscar lit one of Jack's cigarettes. "You don't know about us. Nobody does. You ever see a man fished from the water covered with oil? Eyeballs like fisheyes. You're lucky you're in a plane. Clean, up there in the clouds, nice."

When Jack left the bar the lights on the street were dancing in his eyes. He was numb all over. He walked up and down the streets. *Dotty. Can't talk to her now. Drunk.* He went under the boardwalk and fell down on the cold damp sand. The moon on the ocean broke up in a million sparks. He hung over the rocks throwing up. *Never going to drink again.* His throat burned. *Never . . . never. . . .* He dug his shoes in the sand to

clean them. He smelled. He was ashamed to go back
to the Espositos till late that night.

Another day passed in the same aimless way. Then
on the seventh day of his furlough, his last day in New
York, Jack plucked up his courage and walked to
Dotty's house. She lived in a tall white elevator building. He stood across the street, then walked around
the block again. What a fool he was! The time had
just gone, slipped away. No, it was all excuses. He
was scared. Plain scared.

He walked into a phone booth. Dialed. It was so
stupid. What was the use of calling now when he had
to leave that night. The phone was answered immediately. "Dotty?" he said.

"Just a minute, I'll get her."

His knees were shaking. "Hello," Dotty said.

"Hello," he said, "it's Jack Raab."

"Jack! Where are you?" He told her. "That's right
around the corner," she said. "Stay right there. Don't
move! I'll come meet you."

He waited outside the phone booth. She came
around the corner. She was taller than he remembered, and wearing her hair a different way. Her
leopard-skin coat flew open. She looked smart and
sophisticated, a million miles above him. "Hello!" she
said. "Hello, Jack Raab!"

He smiled. He didn't know what to say. "Want to
walk?" he said.

"Great! I like to walk. This way, to the ocean."
They walked along side by side. "Isn't it funny," she
said, "we met at the ocean, and here we are going to
the ocean again." She kept the conversation going.
"I'm so glad my family lives here, I love the ocean.
It's never the same, it's always changing."

"That's right," he said. "That's right." He couldn't think of anything to say. He bumped into her accidentally and jumped away. She looked up at him, smiling.

"My furlough's almost over," he blurted. "I'm going back tonight."

"Tonight!" She looked shocked. "Jack, I thought—" She broke off. "Well, you must have had a million things to do, and people to see."

"Right, right," he said. He felt ashamed. What a phony. "I'm going overseas after this." He was playing for her sympathy. He began hobbling a little bit.

"You hurt yourself," she said.

"It's nothing," he said bravely.

They were on the Boardwalk. They stood looking out over the ocean. Everything was going wrong. He was acting like a jerk. Dotty was leaning on the railing with a little smile on her face. Probably just waiting to get away from him.

"Look—if you want to go back," he said.

A surprised look crossed her face. "Why? Do you have to leave?"

"No! No, not me. I thought maybe you—"

"No," she said, "it's Saturday, no school today, and—"

"Lucky me!" he said. He meant it. "Dotty—the thing is—I was—" He cleared his throat. "Uh—scared—"

"What of?"

"You hardly know me," he said. "I mean, both of us—we hardly know each other."

She linked her arm with his. "I know, that's why I'm glad we have this time." They kept walking. She matched him stride for stride. He felt easier and told her about Corporal Cohen in Miami and how he made Jack march in front of the platoon and then abused him because he was out of step all the time.

"Poor Jack," Dotty said, laughing.

They were both getting hungry. They found a luncheonette under the elevated and ordered toasted cheese sandwiches and malted milks.

Dotty pushed her coat off her shoulders. She was wearing a string of pearls, a blue wool sweater, and a pleated skirt. She looked at Jack's tunic. "What are the wings?"

"Gunner's wings."

"Only the gunners have them?"

"Everyone who flies has wings," he said. "They all look pretty much alike, but the center is different." He pointed to his stripes. "I'm a sergeant now." He showed her his sharpshooter medal and good-conduct ribbon.

"Are you scared about going overseas?"

He started to shake his head, then he said, "I don't know, Dotty . . . I guess I am partly." He wasn't thinking about combat, though. It was his family— he was going away without seeing them, and that scared him.

Dotty sipped up the last of her malted. They kept talking. No one bothered them. They sat there for several hours. Jack had never spent so much time with a girl. He wanted to say something, to tell her how much he liked her.

"Dotty . . ."

"Yes, Jack?"

"It's really nice—" He stumbled. She waited, her chin in her hands. He looked around. "I want to tell you . . . I mean being here . . . yes, seeing you! It's hard to believe," he said, fast. "It's so nice, I can hardly believe it."

"I feel the same way, Jack."

When they left there were long shadows on the ground. They walked slowly. He wanted to hold her hand, but he didn't. In front of her apartment building she said, "Want to come in?"

He didn't have that much time. He had to get to Penn Station. He looked at his watch. "I'll go up with you, then I have to leave."

"It's hard to believe you're going tonight," Dotty said as they walked into the building. "And that you'll be going overseas."

The elevator was coming. What if he kissed her on the elevator? They got in. They were alone. "Eighth floor," she said, pushing the button. She had dimples in both cheeks like the ice skater Sonja Henie. "Do you ice skate?" Jack said.

"Sure," she said. They both watched the metal pointer. What if he stopped the elevator, grabbed her, and kissed her? "Here we are," she said. The elevator doors slid open. He followed her out into the hall, swinging his shoulders, strutting like a rooster. Dotty looked at him. He hated himself because he couldn't control the way he was acting.

They stopped in front of her door. He wanted to kiss her, and he wanted to give her something. He hadn't brought her a present. Chuckie had brought his girl a miniature set of wings. Jack had thought about it, but that was all.

He removed the Star of David from around his neck. "Dotty—this is for you."

She held it in the palm of her hand. "Jack, are you sure?"

"Yes, I want you to have it. Please—"

She put it around her neck. "Good-bye, Jack," she said, "take care of yourself. Take good care of yourself."

It was the way she said it—it made him feel sad for himself, and older. And then they kissed. He didn't know how it happened. He moved, and she moved. He reached out, she reached out at the same moment. And they were kissing.

He thought he was doing everything wrong. But she was kissing him back. Her hand was behind his head. Oh, it was a kiss, a real kiss, a wonderful kiss!

When they separated she looked altogether different to him. So beautiful. He didn't want to stop looking at her. He felt wonderful. He'd kissed her. He'd kissed Dotty.

"I'll write you," she said. "As soon as I have your overseas address."

He backed away down the hall, not taking his eyes from her. "Good-bye," he said. "Good-bye, Dotty." He was going. It wasn't just a little good-bye. He was going overseas. It was something more final, more important. "Good-bye. . . ." She stood there until he stepped into the elevator.

PART II

THE MISSIONS

The Army Air Corps
(Official song of the United States Army Air Corps)
(Words and music by Robert Crawford, 1939, 1942.)

———

Off we go into the wild blue yonder,
Climbing high into the sun;
Here they come, zooming to meet our thunder,
At 'em boys,
Give 'er the gun! (Give 'er the gun now!)
Down we dive, spouting our flame from under,
Off with one helluva* roar!
We live in fame
Or go down in flame
(SHOUT!) Nothing'll stop the Army Air Corps!

6

Jack opened his eyes the moment Wolpe, the orderly-room clerk, entered the hut. Wolpe was bundled up in a sheepskin-lined flight jacket. It was a cold morning. He flicked on the lights. "Eustice," he read from the list in his hand, "Gonzalez, Johnson, O'Brien, Raab, and Pratt." Nobody stirred. "Breakfast at four thirty, briefing at five thirty, take off at six thirty. Rise and shine, shitheads." Then he was gone.

They'd been in England for ten days, assigned to the Eighth Air Force, 398th Bomb Group, at the Northumberland Air Base. The night before they'd been put on alert for their first mission. Lieutenant Martin told them to get a good night's rest. "Tomorrow's the big one," he said. "Number One."

Jack felt as if he'd hardly slept. He was excited and scared. No use trying to hide it. He was scared, all right. If only it were his second mission, he knew he wouldn't feel this way. All these months, all that impatience. Now it was happening and he wished they'd scrub the mission.

He watched the Nissen hut's single light bulb sway back and forth. The hut was like an icebox. Drops of water glistened on the underside of the curved sheet-metal roof.

At the other end of the hut Wiggins and the other five guys in that crew had gone back to sleep. Ever since they'd arrived, Wiggins had been ragging them, telling them what a green, sad-assed crew they were, and how they'd all be crying for their mommas the first time they saw flak or a plane get hit. Wiggins's crew had already flown eighteen missions.

Fred Pratt was the first one out of the sack, bare-legged in his shorts, poking at the cold fire in the stove. "Damned dead fire!" Fred never swore. Was he scared, too? Jack didn't like it. He wanted Old Man Pratt to be calm.

"Shut the hell up!" Wiggins sat up in his bunk. "What are you screwing around the fire for? You greenies better get out of here, or you'll miss chow, and it's a long time to lunch."

Jack swung out of bed. Bare feet on icy concrete floor. Concrete floors, metal walls, no heat—whoever dreamed up these Nissen huts was a fiend. He dressed quickly. All his clothes were clammy. Everyone was getting up now. Eustice stood shivering, a blanket around his shoulders.

"Where's that skinny spic?" he stammered. "Gonzalez, get your ass in motion."

Dave's head came up like a snake's. "Worry about yourself, hillbilly."

Jack used to think Billy and Dave hated each other, but in their own way they were friends.

"What are we supposed to wear today?" Dave said. He crawled out of his bunk.

Johnson, who slept near the door, shook snow out of his boots. "Your Army-issue long-johns with the quick release bottom."

Jack shook Chuckie. "Okay," Chuckie mumbled, but his eyes were tightly closed. "Plenty of time."

Jack ran out to the latrine, towel around his neck, soap dish and toothbrush in his hand. Like summer camp, except for this icy black night. He splashed water on his face, then dried himself fast and raced back to the hut.

Chuckie was pulling on his boots. His face was still wrinkled with sleep. He tied up his boots slowly, as if he were just coming awake.

Jack and Chuckie were the last ones out of the hut, Wiggins's parting words echoing after them. "Turn out the light, you morons."

They made their way through the blackness. Not a star overhead. The chow hall was blacked out on the outside. Inside it was warm and smelled of coffee and frying eggs. The flying crews were the only ones who got real eggs. Everyone else got powdered eggs.

They ate silently and watched the other more experienced crews stroll in. "Nobody's worried except us," Jack said.

"Who's worried?" Johnson said. But a moment later when Billy and Dave started picking at each other, Johnson exploded. "Why don't you two knock it off! Save it for the Germans!"

The enlisted men's briefing room was crowded and noisy. Everyone was smoking. The air was blue. Jack and his crew sat in back. In front of the room on a raised platform was a map of Europe covered with a white curtain.

When the briefing officer pulled the curtain aside, Jack focused on the long red thread that ran across the map of Europe. That was their mission. A shiver went through Jack.

"Berlin." The word seemed to fly around the room even before the officer said it.

"Berlin," Chuckie repeated, looking at Jack. "Holy Mary." It was the worst target they could have gotten.

"This is going to be the biggest attack we've ever launched against Berlin," the briefing officer said. "You can expect intense antiaircraft fire. The Germans will do everything they can to protect their capital city."

Berlin, Jack thought. Every time he focused on where they were going, he got a jolt in his belly. *Berlin*. That was where Hitler was. Maybe one of the bombs from their plane would be the one to blow Hitler into hell.

They were silent when they left the briefing room. The silence carried over to the equipment room, where they put on their electric-heated suits, zipped up their flying coveralls, and put on their sidearms— .45 revolvers in leather holsters—under their new leather jackets, in case they had to bail out. The Germans were shooting parachuting American airmen.

Jack flung flying helmet, rubber Mae West, sheepskin-lined boots, into the truck along with the chutes and harnesses, then climbed in.

Bombers were dispersed around the field. The ground crew was still loading the bombs into their plane. Jack jumped off the truck, threw his equipment into the waist hatch, then went up the side of the plane to check the wing gas tanks.

It was cold on the wing. He felt the weight of the .45 under his arm. He couldn't forget it. It was too real. They were going out on a mission, but nobody was talking about it, and Jack didn't either.

Outside, Martin spoke to the crew briefly. "We're flying right wing in the high squadron. I'm going to keep this ship as tight in formation as I can. You all know what you have to do. As for the rest of it—" He gestured. "Here's wishing *Godfathers, Incorporated* luck." They had named their plane on the way over after a big discussion. The only name they could all agree on was *Godfathers*, because they were all godfathers to Pratt's little daughter.

Chuckie and Dave crossed themselves, and so did Lieutenant Seppetone. Then the three officers and Pratt, who was the nose gunner and toggled the bombs as well, swung up into the nose. Jack remained outside to help Eustice pull the props through to get the oil circulating. He looked up where the ship's name was lettered. GODFATHERS, INC. A ground crew guy had done the lettering and painted in a baby wearing a diaper and pulling a bomb behind him on a string, like a toy wagon.

"Start one!" Jack stood clear as the engines started. The cowling shook, then belched smoke; the engines roared. The ground crew chief stood by with a fire extinguisher as the engines revved up. Jack ducked under the wings to pull the wheel chocks, then, whipped along by the prop wash, he climbed into the waist hatch and distributed the flak suits: chest and back-protecting armored vests.

As soon as the red flares went up, they started to

roll, part of a procession of bombers lumbering slowly toward the runway. At the same moment all over England other planes from the Eighth Air Force were taking off. B-17's and B-24's, and their fighter escorts, P-51's and P-38's. An armada of more than a thousand planes going into the air.

Jack snapped on the parachute harness and snugged up the straps. He swallowed hard several times. His throat was dry. He put on his flying boots, leaving his shoes and parachute near the starboard gun. For the takeoff he and Paul and Dave all went forward to the radio room and sat on the floor with their backs braced against the metal partition. Chuckie rubbed Jack's head for luck.

Bombers were taking off every ten seconds. The roar of the engines rose to a nearly unbearable pitch. Then they were rolling down the runway, accelerating hard. Jack felt the weight of the bombs slogging around on the other side of the partition.

The wheels bounced. The plane rose laboriously. Fully loaded, the plane carried thirty tons of bombs, guns, ammunition, and fuel. *Up, up,* Jack urged. His body was taut, his legs stiffened. The engines seemed to shake the ship apart. Slowly the plane lifted and rose through a gray bank of clouds.

Jack went back to his position, glanced at the oxygen gauges, the ammo boxes, and the way the shells were feeding into the guns. He looked out the port and then the starboard window for other bombers that might come too close. He kept swallowing to clear his ears. They climbed out of the grayness and into a beautiful blue sky. Under them the clouds looked like fields of snow in the sun.

All around in that blue sky silver bombers rose and

wheeled in great circles, the black First Division triangles on their rudders. Round and round they flew, forming squadrons, then joining into groups and still larger wings. Vapor trails steamed from their engines and wing tips. They were stacked up above and below *Godfathers, Inc.* like stairs, every step bristling with guns.

Through holes in the cloud cover Jack caught a glimpse of London below. He saw bomb craters, raw ugly gashes in the land. They started slowly toward the North Sea and continental Europe. Over the English Channel, Lieutenant Martin gave the order to the gunners. "Arm your guns."

Jack fed a shell into the chamber of the port gun, then crossed over and armed the starboard gun.

A moment later Martin ordered, "Clear your guns."

Jack fired a brief burst from each gun. All the other guns on the plane were firing. The vibrations and the acrid smell of gunpowder excited Jack.

At ten thousand feet the order came through to put on their oxygen masks. Now there were no more faces, only the green snouts of the masks, and the helmets and goggles over them.

Holding the gun, feeling its weight, helped Jack stay calm. Over the engine's steady roar he heard other sounds. Berlin . . . Berlin . . . Berlin . . . like a tuneless piece of music. Below he saw the water of the North Sea, and then the coast of Holland and the Zeider Zee. No signs of fighter planes, either their own or enemy.

At twenty thousand feet Dave called from the ball, "Flak low at three o'clock." Jack had been looking out the port waist. He swung quickly to the starboard and saw the flak, antiaircraft shells, bursting below them. Smudgy dark stuff. Too far below to be damaging, but there it was, his first flak. It didn't seem real.

They climbed to twenty-five thousand feet. The temperature dropped as they climbed. Jack adjusted the thermostat on his electric suit. The slow ponderous flight continued. One hundred seventy miles per hour was the B-17's maximum speed under full load. It was peaceful, nothing was happening. Jack reminded himself that they were over enemy territory. That, too, seemed unreal.

He pulled the rubber mask away from his face and let the moisture from his breath drain from around his chin. He leaned on the gun, looking up and down, then crossed to his other position and searched the sky again. He was waiting . . . waiting for something to happen . . . waiting to see if he'd be scared.

Hours passed. His heavy flak suit was breaking his back. He checked periodically to see if his lifelines were connected—the electric intercom, the oxygen. He checked the red ball on the oxygen regulator, then cracked the ice puddling around his chin under the rubber mask. The air seeping through the waist was like ice.

Suddenly Eustice's voice cracked over the intercom. "Fighter planes at two o'clock high." His turret was on top of the plane, right behind the pilots. "Fighter planes, fighter planes!"

"Slow down, Billy," Lieutenant Seppetone said.

"I see them," Eustice cried, his voice higher than ever. "They're like little tiny black things!"

Jack slung his gun around and looked up. The sun's rays blinded him.

"Hold your fire," Lieutenant Martin ordered from the cockpit. "They're ours."

Damn! That crazy Eustice. He had spotted their own fighters, the P-51 Mustangs that were escorting the bombers over Germany. Sweat trickled down Jack's face.

"I keep telling you, Billy," Dave cackled over the intercom, "you should have joined the Luftwaffe."

"Okay, button up," Lieutenant Martin broke in. "We're approaching the Initial Point. I don't want any more chitchat on the intercom."

Jack moistened his lips. The Initial Point was the start of the bomb run. From here to the target the enemy fire was the heaviest. There was no changing altitude now to throw off the enemy antiaircraft, no dodging flak. The bomb run ran straight and true as a railroad track until the bombs were dropped.

Ahead Jack could see the planes beginning to bank to the right, wings tipped. Berlin was directly ahead, a great expanse of brown like a rusted iron waffle. Smoke filled the air as the German antiaircraft gunners found their level. Puffs of dirty gray smoke. Shells fragmented in midair. They didn't look dangerous, but Jack knew they were full of bits of jagged metal that could tear a man apart.

Their bombers were dumping bags of silver chaff to confuse the German radar. The flak climbed up steadily. Jack pulled a flak suit around himself and crouched over his gun. There was a thickness behind his eyes, a weight at the back of his head.

The moment they entered the bomb run they were buffeted by prop wash and by flak that hit like gravel being flung against a tin roof. The plane jerked and bolted. This is it, Jack said to himself. This is the worst part. It isn't going to get any worse. His heart was beating frantically. He sank down behind his gun so he had the full protection of the ship's armor. He couldn't control himself. He was crouched down, bent over double, bent over around himself, protecting himself.

Get up, he ordered himself. He was horrified to find himself crouched over that way. *Get up.* He forced himself up. He made himself straighten up. And as he did, he saw a bomber snap in half. The tail section spun slowly toward the earth. Then a man fell out of the plane, and another, and another. He counted four chutes. Where were the rest? More things were happening than he could register.

Smoke filled the air. A plane drifted gracefully out of formation, two engines trailing twin tails of smoke. Pieces of planes flew through the air. A wing darted by. Then the shadow of something dark fell so close to Jack's position he ducked. Only after it passed did he realize it was a man falling through the air.

"Drop the bombs," Johnson screamed. "What the fuck are you waiting for?"

"Get the fuck off the line," Martin shouted.

Fred Pratt had to wait for the bombardier on the lead ship. Pratt wasn't a bombardier, just a gunner who let the bombs go. A bombardier used a bomb-sight to aim at the target. Fred just watched the lead ship. When it dropped its bombs, Fred dropped theirs.

On and on they went. The bomb run was only minutes long, but it went on forever. Jack crouched and watched and waited for the bombs to go. Waited and waited. No enemy aircraft. Just that flying flak blowing them up.

Ahead he saw bombs drop from under the planes, strings of eggs falling. "Bombs away," Pratt shouted.

Godfathers, Inc. leaped up as the bombs were released. It seemed to go wild with relief.

Martin banked the plane sharply away from the target. The right wing dipped. Clinging to his gun, Jack looked out at the thick oily columns of smoke rising from the earth. Berlin on fire. He didn't think of what lay below, or what they'd done. They'd dropped the bombs, that was all he cared about.

The flak thinned out. Behind them Jack counted seven crippled bombers falling back, unable to keep up with the tight layered formations. Now the enemy planes would appear to pick off the cripples one by one.

Lieutenant Martin came on the intercom, talking fast. "Everyone okay? I want a report from every position. Stay on the alert, we're still over enemy territory. Any emergencies? Anyone hurt? Oxygen okay? Check your gauges. Did we take any flak?"

"There's one hole up here big enough to put your ass through," Fred Pratt announced from the nose. He sounded like himself again.

There was a tightness in Jack's throat, a limp heavy feeling in his knees. Was it over? It was almost over. The worst was over. Had he done all right? One moment of uncontrollable fear, then he had been all right. He was glad nobody had seen him.

The trip back felt half as long as the trip in. Jack sang over the sound of the engines. "Off we go, into the wild blue yonder! Flying high . . . into the SUN!" Over the English Channel he unhooked his flak suit. At ten thousand feet, when they reached the coast of England, he pulled off the oxygen mask and lit a cigarette. It tasted awful, but he smoked it down to nothing. It was just good to smoke. Below he saw the white cliffs, the breakers boiling in. The white cliffs of Dover, just like the song. "There'll be blue birds over the white cliffs of Dover," he sang. "Tomorrow, just you wait and see. . . ."

When the plane touched down, Jack was ready to go. Out of his flying clothes, harness, electric suit, and into his shoes. He had his guns cleared, the ammo in the ammo boxes. The moment they rolled to a stop and the engines were cut, he was out of the plane.

It was late afternoon, a gray day. They'd been in the air for over nine hours. Jack's head rang from the sound of the engines. Squatting down, he rubbed his hands over the ground. He was back. He was safe. He'd flown his first mission. Dirt had never felt so good.

7

The missions piled up. Hamburg . . . Kassel . . . Munich. . . . Their fifth mission was over Bremen. "Flak at three o'clock low," Dave said from the ball. "Coming up like shit up the stairs."

Jack squatted, arms together, knees up, making himself as small as he could. He'd thought after the first mission they would get easier and easier, but just the opposite had happened. Before every mission he was nervous, jumpy, he couldn't eat, and never got enough sleep.

Even when they weren't flying, he was thinking about it. Eating a meal, enjoying the food, but in the back of his mind thinking this could be the last time he'd eat, the last swallow of milk, the last piece of bread. In a sense every second had become the last second.

Billy had it just as bad as Jack. Jack had thought Billy didn't have a nerve in his body—always that soft smile, that round white bland face—but poor Billy was throwing up his breakfast every morning behind the plane. And Johnson was shaking so bad he had to hang on to his coffee cup with both hands.

"Bomb bay doors open." The bomb run was beginning. Jack dragged the extra flak suits around his feet and hooked the chest chute to one shackle of his harness. Then he cleared the ice from his mask and glanced at the oxygen gauge, for a moment breathing the thin lifeless four-mile-up air.

Outside, the silver ships bounced and bobbed, and swung out and then back into position. Now wasn't the time to think. Everything in him was in suspension. He saw the flak, gray black smudges dirtying the sky. His stomach knotted. Riding into the flak was like riding a train out of the light and down a dark tunnel. They were going straight down the rail. Just riding in and taking it till the bombs were dropped.

Shells burst under the ship. The plane shuddered, then there was a sound like a giant garbage can slamming up against them. Jack felt it in the soles of his feet. Then nothing. Waiting again, his balls shriveling. The skin of the ship was too thin. The flak was hitting the plane all over. Jack put his gloved hands over his crotch and burrowed into himself like a turtle.

"Bombs away," Pratt yelled. It was like a commutation of a death sentence. The bombs dropped, and the plane leaped as if steel bands had been severed. Jack grabbed for a hold as Martin dipped the wing, then banked steeply away from the target. The earth swung below his eyes. They were past the target. The flak was behind them. They'd come through again.

"Everybody okay?" Everyone was coming in on the

intercom now, all talking at once. It was always this way after the bomb run. "Did you see that flak?"

"See it? I felt it go right through me."

There was a scattering of uneven holes in the side of the ship. They might have been punched out with an ice pick. It was then Jack noticed that the leg of his tan flight coveralls was scorched. And there, less than an inch from his feet, he saw the piece of flak that had done the damage.

He picked it up, a twisted piece of metal hardly bigger than his thumb. The jagged little destroyer could have torn his knee apart, or worse. It filled him with amazement and dread. This was the garbage that was always coming at them, whispering and whistling and sliding and rattling through the plane.

This was just one fragment, one tiny piece of metal. It had come close, too close. It had been deflected by the armor under his feet. Pure luck. Chance. Accident. This was the one that had missed.

But even knowing how close it had come, there was a feeling in Jack that it could never have got him anyway. A feeling that nothing could really hurt him. He was one of the lucky ones—he and Chuckie. He didn't believe they could die. But it scared him all the same.

When they reached the North Sea he crawled forward to show the fragment of flak to Chuckie in the radio room. Chuckie had his mask off. They were below ten thousand feet. The mask had left a red mark around his face. He removed his earphones, hefted the flak, turned it over in his hand. He looked at the burned spot on Jack's coveralls. "Jesus, buddy, that could have been it."

"Never touched me," Jack said. He didn't want
Chuckie to think he was scared, but he couldn't stop
talking about the flak. "I felt it," he said. "It was like
someone kicked me in the knee. I felt it hit."

That wasn't the only flak they'd taken. After they
landed they counted seventeen flak holes in the ship.

Later, while they waited with Wiggins and the other
guys for the debriefing officer, a clerk brought in two
trays, each holding nine shot-glasses of cognac.

Lieutenant Turner, a tall balding guy, toasted both
crews. "Good job, guys. Here's how." Not everyone
drank. Dave, Eustice, and Milt Held never touched
the stuff.

Jack swallowed his cognac fast. It still tasted like
medicine. And after not eating all day, Jack felt it hit
his stomach like a mule. "I'm drunk," Chuckie said.
"Are you drunk?"

"Who, me?" Jack fell into Chuckie's arms as if his
legs were spaghetti.

By the time the debriefing officer appeared, everyone was sprawled out and relaxed. Martin had his hat
tipped over one eye, and Lt. Seppetone was fast asleep.

The debriefing officer wore a starched tunic. "Here
comes Lieutenant Chickenshit," Chuckie muttered to
Jack. The debriefing officer looked them over, then sat
down. What could he say? They were flying combat,
and he was only an office commando.

The debriefing was thorough, covering the weather,
the route, enemy fire, and bombing results. The officer
made notes on everything to go into the official records.

The next time they flew Jack took the piece of flak
with him. Wiggins, from the other crew in their hut,
told him, "Anything that comes that close and doesn't

hit you has got to be good luck." They'd gotten friendly with Wiggins's crew. They played darts and drank
together in the pub in Royston, a nearby village.

The piece of flak became part of the junk Jack
carried with him on every flight. Besides the flak,
there was a big English penny, his silver Zippo lighter,
and a picture of his parents that he'd taken with him
when he left home. Dotty had sent him pictures, too.
There was one of herself in a bathing suit, and one
sitting on a park bench. He had her pictures tacked
up on the door of his locker in the Nissen hut.

Dotty was writing him every week. He kept the thin
blue sheets of V-mail in an empty English biscuit tin.
If Dotty's letters were a day or two late Jack became
moody. He began carrying her latest letter along with
him, as part of his luck, just like his piece of flak and
his scorched coveralls.

Everyone had something he considered lucky.

Billy wore the same clothes, even the same pair of
socks, the same underwear, for every mission. As far
as Jack knew, Billy never washed them, just took
them off and hung them in his locker for the next
mission.

"You know what that stuff smells like?" Johnson
said one time. "Two-month-old elephant shit."

"Mind your own business, asshole. Just leave my
stuff alone."

Everyone was jumpy. You didn't joke around about
another guy's lucky pieces. Nobody knew what would
work, so anything could be used. Dave carried a Bible
in his pocket, and Chuckie wore a red baseball cap.
One was just as important as the other.

* * *

It was the end of February. They didn't fly every
day, but then, depending on the weather, they might
fly four or five days straight. Every mission left Jack
more tired than the one before. He'd drop off to
sleep like falling off the edge of a cliff. Then, almost
instantly it seemed, someone would be shaking him.
"No . . ." He hadn't slept enough.

"We're flying this morning."

"No . . . lemme sleep." He wanted to sleep, he'd
never wanted anything so much.

"Up and at 'em." It was Old Man Pratt. "You don't
want to miss."

Wearily, still half asleep, he'd pull on his flight
pants. It would be the middle of the night. Icy cold.
He'd bolt down a cup of coffee and a piece of toast.
He had no appetite. Then into the air, and hour after
hour nothing but the roar of the engines, and the
plane shaking, rattling his teeth in his head. Never a
moment when he could let down, and never a moment
when the fear wasn't there with him in the back of
his mind or deep in his belly.

Mission number twelve was Essen in the industrial
Rhine section. The flak was heavy. They went in,
dropped their bombs, and got out. Everything went
well until Chuckie checked the bomb bay and reported a bomb still hanging by one shackle. It was a
bad situation. A five-hundred-pound bomb banging
against the side of the ship. It had never happened
before. It felt like bad luck.

The drag from the open bomb bay doors was slowing them down. They dropped back, losing their pro-
tected position in the squadron. Lieutenant Martin
came on the intercom. "Get the damned thing out of
there, Jack!" In the radio room Chuckie's head jerked

up. Jack hooked on an emergency oxygen bottle and went forward.

When he opened the door, the wind roared up through the open bomb bay. He saw the yellow five-hundred-pounder hanging by one shackle. Below, nothing but wide open sky. He clung to the guide wires over the catwalk and didn't look down. The plane rocked from side to side. It was clumsy work inching along the walk in his flight boots. The oxygen bottle kept banging against his side.

A ground-crew artist had painted a Kilroy-Was-Here face on the side of the bomb—two big eyes and stiff hair sticking up over the side of a fence. Jack leaned over the bomb and pried free the trigger release on the shackle. The bomb dropped. For a moment it seemed to float at the edge of the bomb bay, then it dropped and disappeared against the brown face of Germany.

Jack crawled back into the plane. His hands were shaking as he plugged in his intercom, the electric lines, and the main oxygen line. "Waist gunner to pilot, over. Bomb released."

"Everything okay, Jack?"

Jack swallowed. He started to speak—"Okay"—Then he shut up. He'd done his job. He didn't want to say anything. He could have fallen out of the plane.

"Tail gunner to waist," Paul broke in over the intercom. "Hey, Ace, I think you hit a Nazi command post under an outhouse. You caught them with their pants down."

Jack leaned against his gun. He was still shaking. Let Paul go forward next time! He held the mask away from his face and nibbled a chocolate bar. There were pains in his knees and shoulders. Maybe growing pains. He could feel the knobs of his knees through all the layers of his clothes. He was growing bonier every day. He felt tired, just tired. It was the way he felt all the time.

8

"You want a beer?" Chuckie said.

Jack nodded. "Mild and bitter."

"Two 'af-and-'afs," Chuckie said to the barmaid. "And two meat pies." He and Jack were in the Royston village pub, Ducks and Drakes. Jack slumped down with his head in his hands. "What's the matter with you?" Chuckie said.

"Nothing," Jack said. "I watched the mission coming back from Kassel today."

"What were you doing on the flight lines?"

"I saw a flare and hitched a ride over." The red flare meant either the plane was in trouble, or somebody aboard was hurt.

"That was stupid," Chuckie said. "You have a day off, stay away from them."

"They had this guy wrapped in a blanket," Jack said.

"Stop thinking about it," Chuckie said.

"Even his face was covered."

"Dead?" Chuckie asked.

"As good as dead. Kapstein, the ground crew chief, told me the guy didn't have a face anymore."

"Jesus," Chuckie said. "I wish you'd stay away from the flight lines, Jack. What's the use of all that?"

Jack shrugged and lit a cigarette. "It could have been someone we know," he said.

Chuckie nodded. "We've been damn lucky." He touched his St. Christopher medal. They hadn't had any wounded. And they'd flown all their missions as a crew. Other crews had had a lot of replacements. It had happened to Wiggins—two or three different pilots. And one of their guys had flown an extra mission with another crew and been shot down over Munich. Nobody knew what had happened to him.

"God is watching over us," Chuckie said.

Jack shook his head. "If he's watching so hard, how come he's letting this war go on? How come this guy had his face blown away?"

"He can't be watching everybody and everything, every second," Chuckie said. "There's a reason for things happening the way they do. God has a reason, but we don't always see it. Anyway, when your time comes, that's it. God takes you to Heaven."

"I don't believe in Heaven," Jack said. "Where is it?" He looked up. "Heaven up there? No way!"

At that Chuckie laughed. "That's true. It's Hell up there."

For eight days after their twelfth mission, they didn't fly. Bad weather, rain and storms over Britain and Europe. Night after night they were put on alert, and Jack would sleep poorly, then in the morning it would be raining, the wind gusting around the Nissen hut, and the mission would be scrubbed.

Several times they had suited up before the mission was scrubbed. And once they were actually in the air, climbing up through thick gray clouds, when they got the word to turn back.

Then the weather cleared. It was the beginning of March. The fields were turning green, and there was an unmistakable fresh smell of spring in the air. For six days straight they flew. The thirteenth mission, the fourteenth, fifteenth, sixteenth, seventeenth, and eighteenth. Berlin again . . . Leipzig . . . Stuttgart . . . Frankfurt . . . Münster . . . Cologne. Every morning, after briefing and breakfast, they went off to war the way other men went to work. It was a job. They delivered bombs the way mailmen delivered letters, and then they went home.

At night Jack dropped into the sack and fell dead asleep. He didn't think, he didn't want to think. But two or three hours later he'd wake up, his heart pounding, sure that his name was being called for the flying roster. *Jack Raab*.

But the room would be dark, everyone asleep. Then for a long time he'd lie there, hearing the engines in the distance on the flight lines, being tuned and revved up by the mechanics for the next day.

It wasn't the war he'd dreamed it would be back home in The Bronx. Then he'd thought he was going to be one of those flying aces zipping around the sky in a fighter plane, shooting down Germans left and right. It hadn't happened that way. He hardly thought about Hitler anymore. It was just the war, day after day, like a foot jammed in his belly. He lived with it. It didn't stop him from being on the alert and watching for enemy planes and the flak they were going to catch. It didn't stop him from singing, hum-

ming over the roar of the engine, composing un-
forgettable masterpieces.

The morning of the nineteenth mission Chuckie
tossed Jack an orange. Lieutenant Seppetone handed
out nine chocolate bars and nine packs of chewing
gum. "This is going to be a long one," Lieutenant
Seppetone said in his sleepy way. They were flying
over Berlin for the third time. Jack was already soaked
with sweat.

The first thing he did when he climbed into the
ship was grab the oxygen mask and suck pure oxygen.
It picked him right up, took the ache out of his bones,
and made him feel alive.

They were carrying four one-thousand-pounders in
the bomb bay, the biggest bombs they'd ever carried.
Godfathers, Inc. rumbled down the runway. It was
still dark. The runway lights kept coming and coming. Blue lights disappearing behind them, and then
the red lights which meant Look out, Charlie, you're
coming to the end of the road. They took off slow and
heavy. After takeoff Jack went back to the waist to
watch for planes. It was going to be a long day. It
was always a long day to Berlin.

He watched the skies for the enemy fighters that
never came. Hour after hour . . . the plane droning
. . . watching empty skies. . . . He heard the sound of
his own breath in his helmet, and beyond that the
steady roar of the engines. His mind drifted. He
thought about Dotty . . . dreamt about seeing her
again. He wouldn't be as slow this time. It seemed
so long ago, and he'd been so young. The guys talked
about women all the time—the women they'd left at
home, the girls they met in the pubs. Billy and Dave

both had girlfriends at home and regular girlfriends in the village.

There was one woman, Evelyn, a WAAF, who liked Chuckie. Anytime Jack and Chuckie were in Ducks and Drakes, Evelyn somehow showed up. She was always smiling. Her blue cap rested in a big yellow head of curls.

"I don't think Margie would mind about Evelyn and me, do you, Jack?" Chuckie said one time. "A few kisses—that's all. I can't help it, but it doesn't mean anything. Evelyn knows that Margie and I are true to each other. I'm true to her, Jack, I'll always be true to Margie."

One day Evelyn brought a friend with her, another WAAF. "Virginia, this Yank is Sergeant Chuckie, and this is his friend, Sergeant Jack."

Virginia was neat and pretty. "Didn't I tell you he was smashing, Virgie?" Evelyn said. "Tall and good looking, but he doesn't talk much, do you, Jack? He's a bit shy."

That "bit shy" stuck with Jack. It was true enough, he hardly got out five words to Evelyn, even though she was very nice. But Dotty was his girl. That was the way he thought about her now.

He dreamt about going home after he'd flown his missions, and seeing her. He imagined the way she would meet him, the way they'd rush into each other's arms and hold each other and kiss and kiss and kiss.

"Fighter, fighter!" Billy's voice over the IC, shrill with excitement. "He's coming, he's coming, ten o'clock high. He's coming right at us."

Jack swung his gun around. His goggles fogged. He tore them off. A black plane with a huge black and white swastika on its rudder swept across their wing tips, then dropped out of sight. A German jet, the first fighter plane he'd seen on all their missions.

Beneath him he felt the plane shake as Dave's guns hammered. The smell of gunpowder filtered through the plane. "Stay alert," Martin ordered over the IC. "He may come back. Who got a shot at him? Jack?"

"I fired," Dave said from the ball. "I had him right in my sights."

"You hit him?"

"I don't know. I think so. Did anyone see smoke?"

Jack ducked across the bay and checked his other gun. The first enemy plane he'd seen, and he'd muffed it. Never even pulled his trigger. He'd just stared, it was so unreal. He'd never seen such a huge swastika.

As they approached the target, bags of silver chaff fluttered from the bombers like Christmas tinsel. Black smoke obscured Berlin. He could see the bomb bursts like bunches of gray flowers.

"What the fuck's the matter with your bombardiers," Johnson said over the IC. "Do it!"

Then they ran into the flak. Explosions like doors being slammed. Gravel hit the plane. Then an explosion that rocked the plane from end to end. The plane shook. Jack saw the prop on number four engine whipping around unevenly. "Feather it," Martin yelled at Lieutenant Held over the IC. "Feather it!"

They were still on the bomb run. The prop on number four engine was still now. They were flying on three engines.

"Bombs away!"

They swung clumsily away from the target. They were slipping out of formation. How bad was it? Jack looked over to the radio room, wishing he could talk to Chuckie. He couldn't leave his position. Nobody was saying anything. Jack checked his parachute. It was hanging from his harness by one shackle.

Martin came on the intercom, talking fast. "Number four engine is out, and we're losing power in three. We're not going to be able to stay in formation. We're going to be on our own. Stay at your positions. Stay sharp. We'll have fighter cover. We've got a good chance of making it."

Jack kept watch. They were crippled, and if that German fighter saw them now, he'd attack. His hands were damp. Funny, he felt calm, but he was sweating like a pig.

All the way across Germany and over Holland a couple of fighter planes, Mustang P-51's, escorted them. *Godfathers, Inc.* kept losing altitude. They dropped so low Jack could see the water and fields, and the roads between the fields. He was sure Martin would take them down in Holland or Belgium, which were in Allied hands. But Martin said they were going back to England. He thought they could make it. He was the captain.

Over the English Channel number three engine went, and they began to lose altitude fast. There was no turning back. "I want everything movable jettisoned," Martin ordered.

In the radio room Chuckie sent out an SOS. Dave came up from the ball and Paul came forward. They helped Jack jettison ammo, guns, flak suits, and the oxygen tanks. Everything loose went, and still they dropped. Jack was startled to see how close the water was. He saw the wind track across the surface, and the lines of whitecaps. Chuckie was still sending out distress ditching signals. "Mayday! Mayday!"

"Forgot my bathing cap," Paul said. The oxygen mask hung by one strap from the side of his helmet. His eyes were sunken in his face. "No swimming trunks, either."

"Christ Jesus," Dave said, "you'll be making jokes when they lower you into the ground."

They braced themselves for the crash against the forward wall of the radio room. Jack had his head down against his knees. He was waiting for the crash. Waiting. He felt as if there were slivers of ice in his chest. They were going to crash. He was pleased to be so calm. There were just those slivers of ice that kept rising in his chest. And he was worried about his head. He locked his hands behind his head. Then they hit.

Jack's head went back against the bulkhead. Everything was flung up in the air. Chuckie fell across Jack's chest. It happened in an instant, and yet it all happened in slow motion. There was blood on Chuckie's face. Dave was half through the bomb bay door. Paul was raising himself to the hatch. Water was rushing in.

Jack didn't remember getting out. Paul was reaching down for him. Jack turned to help Chuckie. The water was above Chuckie's waist.

Outside the wind was blowing. Dave freed the raft from its wing compartment. Martin, hatless, climbed out the pilot's window. He yelled something to Sam Seppetone, who was freeing the forward raft. Jack, Chuckie, Paul, and Dave scrambled into their raft. The waves carried them swiftly from the plane. Their last view of *Godfathers, Inc.* before it disappeared under the water was the black triangle on its tail and the division's letter A.

They had plenty of trouble getting the two rafts lashed together. They were all soaked, and Lieutenant Seppetone had a bruise the size of an egg on his forehead. Dark green waves rose up on all sides. At times they were knee deep in water. The movement of the raft made Jack sick. Up and down the sides of the waves they rode, sliding one way, then another. Dave knelt over the side and threw up.

Chuckie tried to get the kite antenna up for their emergency radio transmitter, but the wind ripped it out of his hand. Lieutenant Seppetone calculated their drift. They'd been close to England when they ditched. The P-51 escorts had followed them all the way down. Pratt had seen them wagging their wings before heading home. "They'll just have to radio our position to Air-Sea Rescue," he said.

When it grew dark the wind died down and the sea quieted. In the other raft no one spoke. Martin hadn't said anything for hours.

Jack was cold and wet. He didn't want to take his hands out from under his jacket. "How's it going?" Chuckie said.

Jack just looked at him. He kept watching for a light, a boat to rescue them. How would anyone find them in this darkness?

What an idot Martin had been to try to bring them home. Poor judgment. He'd taken a chance with all their lives. He could have played it safe, gone down in Belgium, which the Allies held. Why hadn't he? Showing off? Cocky? Jack didn't understand it. Martin was their pilot, he was supposed to think for all of them.

Jack fell asleep sitting up, his legs tangled with Paul's and Chuckie's. Paul woke him. He'd heard something. "You guys hear it?"

They were all alert now, listening. Jack could only hear the water. "I hear it," Dave said. "I hear it!"

"Shh!"

They listened again. Then Jack heard it, too. A deep steady throb. In a moment Chuckie had the Very flare gun ready to signal.

"Hold it," Billy said. "What if they're Germans?"

"Signal," Martin ordered.

Chuckie raised the Very gun. The flare swished up, sparkling pink then red. In its falling light Jack made out the silhouette of a black boat running without lights.

They waited. Friend or enemy, there was nothing to do now but wait. They heard the deep-throated motors approach. There was the sharp clang of metal. Jack's heart raced. What if Billy was right, and they were Germans? Martin had been wrong once.

The motor died down. A light came on, illuminating the rafts. Jack held his hand to his eyes. Then a voice from the darkness—"You the American fliers?" An unmistakable British accent.

"What the hell took you Limeys so long?" Paul shouted. "We're not paying for this ride."

It was an Air-Sea Rescue launch. A ladder was dropped over the side of the boat. Dave went up first. His legs cramped, and he started to fall. "Easy does it, chap!" Somebody caught him under the arms and raised him to the deck. Chuckie was next, then Jack. He smiled at the British sailors, then threw his arms around Chuckie.

9

A week went by after the ditching before they flew again. That same week while their new plane, *Godfathers II*, was being outfitted, Wiggins and the others in their Nissen hut were shipped back to the States. They had completed their thirty-five missions. Jack's crew had completed nineteen. "Sixteen still to go," Billy said.

"Who's counting?" Johnson said.

"Why don't you both shut up," Dave said.

They always avoided talking about the missions left to fly. One at a time, that was the only way. Once you started adding them up, you were fooling with your luck. But they all felt a little depressed. All those empty bunks in the hut. It was as if Wiggins and the others had gone out on a mission and never come back. It was unnaturally quiet. Too much room. Something was missing. Wiggins and his big mouth had become part of Jack's life. The others felt it, too.

The night they were put on alert again they sat

around the hut playing cards and biting at each other.

Dave was up and down, couldn't sit still, going in and out of the hut. "Sit down, you Mexican jumping bean," Billy said.

"Sit down yourself, I'm just checking the weather. We'll be going up for sure."

"What do you want to do, play cards till the war ends?" Paul said.

Chuckie threw down a card. "Shut up, all of you, and play. There's nothing we can do about the weather, nothing we can do about the missions, nothing we can do about anything."

There was a phrase going round and round in Jack's head. *Once your luck breaks, that's it.* They'd been lucky up until the ditching. Maybe the ditching was a warning.

In the middle of the night Jack woke with excruciating stomach cramps. He stumbled out of bed, stuck his bare feet in icy boots, and sat in the latrine with a flashlight and a copy of *Stars and Stripes*, wishing he would die. He had the GI's, diarrhea. When he finally got back to bed, he was shivering, chilled, couldn't get warmed up. He'd hardly dozed off again when the light came on in the hut.

"Rise and shine, shitheads." It was Wolpe, the squadron clerk.

Jack swung out of bed. The moment his feet hit the floor he had to run to the latrine. After he came back he told Chuckie, "Tell Martin I can't fly. I'm making sick call." Jack huddled in bed.

Chuckie patted Jack's head before he left. Jack dozed and woke. Bad dreams. He was clinging to the top of a wall that rose higher and higher. . . . He couldn't get down . . . he was going to fall. . . . He sat up, drenched in sweat. He heard the planes revving up for takeoff. They were leaving him behind.

He looked around the hut. Chuckie's pants stretchers were on the floor, a bottle of Vitalis had tipped over, Billy's Betty Grable pinup was hanging by one tack. Everything was falling apart. Jack had the most awful feeling. He didn't want to be here alone. He rolled out of bed and pulled on his clothes. He shouldn't have let them go without him. He'd upset the way they'd always done things . . . their regular order. . . . He belonged on the plane, they'd never flown without him before. He felt as if everything were in jeopardy, all their lives . . . something would happen . . . their luck would give out, and this time it wouldn't be just a warning. . . . It would be his fault. Because he was here, and not where he belonged.

He ran out; maybe he could catch them. A cramp doubled him over. He ran with his hands over his belly. The air was filled with the roar of engines. He ran, but he only got as far as the latrine.

Later he made sick call. He saw at a glance that the mourners' bench was filled with ground personnel and office commandos. He was the only flying crew personnel there. The medic took his temperature and gave him a pink milky liquid in a paper cup. Jack went back to the empty Nissen hut. All day he ran back and forth to the latrine. Late in the afternoon when it was time for the planes to start coming in, he biked slowly over to the flight lines. He was groggy and a little weak.

A warm wind smelling of earth and manure blew across the fields. Jack leaned the bike against one of the sheds. A small hairless black dog sniffed at his shoes. All day the crew had been on Jack's mind. Who did they get to replace him? Did they take much flak? Were they on their way home? *Were they all right?*

He bent and scratched the dog's ears, and as he did he remembered the smell of sawdust and chocolate from Stalinsky's grocery back home. There was an old black dog at Stalinsky's, a dog like this one who always greeted Jack when he came into the store. It was a world Jack had nearly forgotten . . . the way life used to be. The crowds on Allerton Avenue . . . the smell of bread from the bakery . . . reading the funnies with Marcia . . . his mother's perfume . . . his father's shaven cheeks. . . .

He knelt there, rubbing the dog's ears. He looked around the airfield, the hot black tar, the metal buildings . . . the smell of oil and gas. . . . All *this* was real, so real it made home seem even more distant and inaccessible. Would he ever go back?

As Jack watched the planes drop one at a time to the airfield, his stomach knotted. He saw a bomber land with a hole clean through the tail. Another B-17 shot up a red emergency flare. Wounded aboard. The stragglers were coming in, and still no *Godfathers II*.

More flares went up. The ambulance with the red cross on its roof raced out to the field. A bomber was circling the field. Jack hitched a ride with a gas truck as it went to meet the planes. *Godfathers II* came down just as he got there. Lieutenant Held grinned down at Jack from the cockpit, his broad forehead glistening with sweat.

"Is everyone okay?" Jack shouted.

Lieutenant Held made the okay sign. Then Chuckie dropped from the plane. "Look at the welcoming committee!" he said.

Jack grabbed Chuckie around the neck and kissed
him on top of the head.

Chuckie grinned. "You should have been along,
Jack. It was a milk run all the way!"

At the end of March they flew their twenty-fourth
mission. The intelligence report that morning was that
men bailing out over Berlin were being hung from
telephone poles. Most of the flyers had stopped carrying their sidearms a long time ago. Useless weight. But
that morning after they left the briefing room, they
all put the guns on again.

Jack was aware of the .45 under his arm. The tightness in his chest seemed worse than usual. But despite
the worry and anxiety, the mission passed routinely.
The only thing that happened was that flak knocked
out their brakes and Control landed them on the
field's longest runway.

After that mission everything seemed to stop dead
for a couple of weeks. No missions, nothing but
chickenshit work around the base. Policing up the
area around the Nissen huts, picking up cigarette
butts, and digging ditches.

Dave took pictures of them with their shovels. On
the inside door of his locker Jack tacked up a picture
Dave had of Chuckie and himself, their arms around
each other's shoulders.

It was mid-April. Spring had come to England. In
the west the Allied Armies were closing in on the
Germans. On the east the Russians were advancing
into Germany. As the armies advanced the concentration camps were overrun, and the prisoners liberated.
Jack read about the gassing, the ovens, and saw the

pictures of the stacked naked bodies, the walking skeletons. The Germans had learned how to kill efficiently thousands upon thousands of Jews. Jack could barely look at the pictures. It was worse than anything he'd imagined. Beyond belief or understanding.

They flew a milk run to St. Nazaire, a German submarine base on the French Atlantic coast, the easiest mission they'd ever flown, every inch of the way through Allied territory. Half a day's work, a couple hours out, and they were back in time for lunch.

When they landed everyone was feeling good. Mission twenty-five under their belts—for Jack, the twenty-fourth. Ten more like that, and they were home free, but no one expected the war to last that long. Billy threw his baseball cap up in the air. They played tag all the way to the mess hall.

A new flying crew was at the table with them. Jack set his tray down next to a blond boy who moved over for him. "You guys just come off a mission?" the boy asked.

Jack buttered a roll, and nodded.

"How many missions has your crew flown?"

"Twenty-five."

The boy whistled. "You been over Berlin?"

Jack held up three fingers, then took a swallow of coffee.

"Three times over Berlin?"

"That's right," Jack said, pushing back his chair. "Three times." The way this kid was looking at him was the way he had looked at Wiggins three months ago. This kid was probably four or even five years older than Jack, but his greenness was written all over him.

"See you around," Jack said. He almost said, See you around, kid.

The last week in April, Jack turned sixteen. He'd been in the Army nearly a year. In the latrine he studied his face in the mirror. There were dark patches around his eyes and hollows in his cheeks. He thought he looked older, but he wasn't sure. He knew he felt older. He didn't say a word about his birthday to anyone, but he thought about it all day long.

PART III

BAIL OUT

"Comin' In on a Wing and a Prayer"
(Words by Harold Adamson, music by Jimmy Mc-
Hugh. Robbins Music Corp., 1943.)

———

Comin' in on a wing and a prayer
Comin' in on a wing and a prayer
Tho' there's one motor gone, we can still carry on
Comin' in on a wing and a prayer
What a show, what a fight!
Yes, we really hit our target for tonight!
How we sing as we limp through the air
Look below, there's our field over there
With our full crew aboard and our trust in the Lord
We're comin' in on a wing and a prayer.

10

On the morning of April 25, 1945, Lieutenant Martin's crew suited up for a combat mission to Pilsen, Czechoslovakia. Their target was the Skoda Munitions Works. It was their first mission since the milk run over St. Nazaire ten days earlier.

Jack was uneasy. Why Czechoslovakia? They'd never flown to Czechoslovakia before. Why now? He'd heard all the rumors. The air war was as good as over. The Army was running out of targets for the air crews. Any day now the European war was going to be wound up and then they'd all be sent to the Far East. India, Australia, or maybe China. Every day there was another rumor.

Jack tossed flak suits into the waist, then slid in the boxes of ammunition. Pilsen, Czechoslovakia, was where beer was made. "What're we going to do?" he asked Chuckie. "Blow up beer factories?"

"It's going to be a milk run," Chuckie said. It was what he always said. He slipped his parachute harness over his leather jacket, snapped up the leg bands, then fastened the harness across his chest. "Milk run, milk run, milk run," he sang. "It's going to be a milk run."

Jack slung his harness over his shoulder. "It's been too long between missions," he said. "It's better when we fly every day. Then we don't have to think about what's going to happen."

"Nothing's going to happen," Chuckie said. He kissed his St. Christopher medal, then rubbed the top of Jack's head for luck.

Jack checked the oxygen gauge, the ammo boxes, cleared the guns, and made sure he had enough flak suits around his position. He wanted everything right. They were too close to the end to do anything sloppy. He checked his pocket to make sure he had his lucky flak piece.

"Here's the way I see it," Chuckie was telling Dave in the radio room, "it's got to be a milk run. What do the Germans have left to throw up at us?"

"Flak," Dave said.

"Sure they have planes," Chuckie went on, "but they can't get them off the ground. No fuel, no parts. Can't get any, their lines are cut, the Russians have Berlin surrounded. General Patton is going through Germany like coal down the chute. The Germans are licked. And don't tell me they don't know it."

"Then what are we flying for?" Jack said.

"Beats me," Chuckie answered, his red head disappearing under his helmet. "Same reason we went every other time. Because the Army wants us to."

The engines were fired. *Godfathers II* shook and smoked, then roared to life. They moved slowly toward the runway. The sun was rising. The wings shivered as the plane rumbled down the runway for takeoff.

It was a moment when Jack could never separate himself from the ship. He felt it straining, struggling to rise from the ground. He held his breath, trying to make himself lighter, trying to help the plane into the sky.

As they rose Jack was pushed back, flattened against the partition. They were in the air and climbing. He swallowed to relieve the pressure, then went back to his position and plugged in the intercom and the electric element of his flight suit. He checked his oxygen mask. The lump inside that he carried on every mission had settled in his chest.

The squad assembled at seventeen thousand feet, and they took their position in the group. Outside, through the waist window, Jack saw the Fortresses in their flashing formations.

It was cold. He pulled up the cuffs of his leather gauntlets, then adjusted the thermostat of the electric suit. The groups droned across Europe in their box-like battle formations. Squadron on squadron. Their squadron was in the tail position. They'd be the last ones through the target. By the time they ran the flak the German antiaircraft would be right on them. Not good, but not worth thinking about.

Jack curled his toes in the insulated boots. Inside his helmet he could hear the whisper of his breath, each breath separate and hissing. And beyond the hissing, the constant high whining rush of the wind and the engines. He raised his voice so it matched the sound outside his head, wailing, singing his high monotonous song.

Every mission was like this—droning, waiting, singing, not thinking. Thinking was *verboten*! If you thought about things too much it could drive you crazy. Jack's eyes shifted from the sky, to the wings, to the muzzle of his gun. Waiting . . . looking carefully at the clouds . . . singing . . . waiting. . . .

He checked the opposite bay. His legs were stiff. His knees cracked. He yawned. Beneath the plane he could see the dark land through breaks in the clouds. Curving silver rivers, darker smudges of the cities.

Then, ahead, the first dirty flak bursts.

"Bomb bay doors open."

As they entered the bomb run, Jack automatically crouched at his position and, turtlelike, pulled the flak suits around himself. There was a thickness behind his head. It was always the same—the thickness, the breathlessness, the waiting.

The flak grew heavier, long gray and black streaks that dirtied the sky. Black exhaust belched from the engines. *Godfathers II* shook as it rode the prop wash of the planes ahead.

Jack snapped his chute to one shackle of his harness, glanced at his shoes tied together on the floor. There was a brief exchange over the intercom. "Close the bomb bay doors," Fred called from the nose. The lead bombardier hadn't dropped his bombs. "We've got to go around again."

"The stupid sonofabitch!" Johnson swore.

Jack glanced ahead where the clouds had closed in over the target. They'd never had to go over a target twice before. Not good.

"What the fuck's the matter with you bombardiers," Johnson broke in again. "Drop the damned things so we can get out of here." "Shut up," Martin snapped. "Stay off the intercom."

Jack swallowed hard as they banked steeply around. The sky was blue, then it turned white as they swept through the clouds. They leveled off and continued in a long looping circle back over the target.

"Bomb bay doors open."

Flak popped around them. Something seemed to nudge the plane. One moment Jack was standing, and the next he was off his feet, tossed up, then buried under boxes and flak suits. He pushed his way up, tried to get to his feet, then fell again. The plane was tipped so sharply he couldn't stand upright.

He jabbed the intercom button. Martin was crazy for flying this way. "Waist gunner to pilot, over." No answering crackle over the line. He jabbed the button again. "Waist gunner to pilot." The intercom line was broken. Then he saw that the coupling was torn loose on his oxygen lines. The air he was breathing was lifeless. He tried to stand but fell to his knees.

The plane was going crazy, dipping, sliding, slipping. Jack crawled to the window. The wing was broken right back to number two engine. It was just hanging there, and as Jack looked, it broke free and fell away.

"Waist gunner to pilot, over!" He jabbed the intercom again and again. His hands were shaking. He grabbed the emergency oxygen bottle, but he couldn't make the connection. He crawled forward.

The wind screamed through the radio compartment. There was a hole blown in the side. Chuckie was sitting crookedly across his seat, his feet jammed under the table.

"Chuckie, the wing's shot off," Jack said. He couldn't see Chuckie's face. The mask covered it. "Chuckie." Jack pushed him. Chuckie's head flopped forward. Where the back of his head should have been was just a wet red jelly.

Now Jack saw that he was crawling in blood. His hands and knees were covered with blood. Something skidded under his knee. He looked down at a piece of Chuckie's skull with hair and white stuff still sticking to it.

Jack threw out his hand, hit the wall, then pulled himself toward the rear. Dave was climbing up out of the ball. His mask was gone. His face was black. Jack crawled to the waist hatch. Through the tunnel he could see the tail position. Paul was gone.

Clumsily Jack pulled the red emergency hinge releases on the hatch door. He was lightheaded, passing out. No air to breathe. He yanked the hinge free. The door hung there. It was supposed to drop out when the hinges were pulled.

Jack looked around. Behind him Dave was clipping on his chest pack. In the doorway to the radio room he saw Chuckie's arm. He had to get out. He *had* to get out. He checked his chest pack, glanced at the red rip cord, then threw himself against the hatch door. It gave way beneath his weight. He fell backward out of the plane.

11

The wind caught Jack and slammed him against the side of the plane. Pinned him there. He didn't fall. He was pressed against the side of the plane. The tail section was over his head. *You're hanging outside the plane.* He was talking to himself as if he were an observer watching what was happening to someone else.

You're stuck to the plane. Maybe this was the way it happened. First you rolled against the side of the plane, then you let go. Only the flight goggles caught over his mouth bothered him, and the way his leg was hooked in the door. He was hanging there by one leg like a stunt man. Everything was happening in seconds, and fractions of seconds, but they were impossibly long seconds. Each second seemed to go on and on, endlessly. Like his leg in the door. It was only caught there a second or two, but it seemed longer, much longer, as if his leg had always been caught in the door.

The wind pressed like arms around him. It was morning, but everything was dim and gray, as if night were coming. *Maybe you're passing out from lack of oxygen*. Then he was afraid suddenly, not about falling through the air with his leg pinned to the plane, but that he'd die there. He didn't want to die. He kicked out with both legs . . . and fell free.

You're falling. It didn't feel like falling. Not what he thought falling should feel like. It was like lying on a soft mattress with the wind pushing through his arms. There was a thin white grayish stuff all around him. Not fluffy like clouds, but not empty space either. He was alone in this grayness. The plane had disappeared. No other planes in sight. No other falling objects. He was alone.

He was calm. Yes, he was sure he was calm. He was aware of everything—the position of his body (he was falling on his back), the pain in his ears, the goggles whipping against his face. Of course it was the first time he'd ever jumped from a plane, but he was calm. He hadn't even pulled the rip cord on his chute yet.

It was good to free-fall. It was good to get away from the falling plane. They'd been up nearly four miles when they were hit. The air was too thin to breathe. It was good to drop down to where the air wasn't so thin.

Jack kept straining to look over his shoulder. He was falling on his back. He wanted to see where he was going. He started to count as he fell into thicker clouds. Gray clouds billowed up all around him. He couldn't see anything. It was annoying.

One hundred . . . two hundred. . . . Was he counting too fast? *Count to a thousand by hundreds before you pull the rip cord.*

Three hundred . . . four hundred . . . five. . . . How far had he fallen? How close was the ground? Was it there, just under these clouds?

Six hundred . . . Seven hundred. . . .

He tried to turn himself so he could see the direction he was going. The wind dug into his eyes. He wanted desperately to see. The goggles beat against his cheek. The pain in his ears was like needles.

Seven hundred . . . eight hundred. . . . It was good to wait. He was calm. It was good to be calm.

A free-falling object from a speeding airplane actually slows down as it falls, lessening the strain on the opening chute.

If you pulled your chute too soon, you'd rip yourself to shreds. *Nine hundred . . . one thousand. . . .*

The parachute handle was on the right side of his chest pack. A red handle. *Reach for it, pull it.* Something big and bulky, like a basket of laundry, slapped up against Jack's face. The chute snapped open. He blacked out.

When he came to, he was hanging suspended from his harness, which was attached by two straps to a leash of ropes tied to a broad white canopy. And under this canopy he was floating gently back and forth beneath a perfect blue-and-white sky. It was a mild spring day. He had fallen out of the dark into the light.

There was a terrible pain in his ears. He swallowed hard to release the pressure. The harness straps dug into him. His crotch was on fire. He lifted himself up on the twin canvas straps, trying to ease the pain, but he could only hold on for a second or two.

The earth was a long way below. No planes in the sky. He looked around. They'd all flown away and left him here. He saw another parachute in the distance. Too far away to see who it was. And still another chute above him. Maybe the one in the distance was Paul. And above him, Dave.

Chuckie. . . . Was he really dead? And the others —Martin, Eustice, Held, Pratt, Seppetone—they couldn't all be dead. Maybe he'd jumped too soon. Maybe Martin had landed the plane safely. Maybe Jack had dreamed the whole thing. Maybe he was dreaming right now. But the pain in his groin was too real. He pulled himself up again on the shrouds.

He was floating through a pretty blue picture-postcard world. A perfect calendar picture, only marred by a long dirty smudge down the edge. That black smear was Pilsen, the burning target.

The ground rose up. Brown fields. Squares of brown, earth colors, shades of gray and green like the blocks of clay he had played with years ago. Black roads and silver streams, and thick uneven patches of pale green woods.

The first spray of bullets was like pebbles whisking by his ears. Little pinging sounds. He thought it was his ears popping. He didn't think they were shooting at him. It didn't even sound like real guns. Nothing like the hard steady hammering of the .50 caliber machine guns.

Little hollow popping sounds. Jack could barely make them out at first. It was like insects buzzing around his ears. He looked up. He saw the tiny holes peppered across the canopy. He could see the sky through the holes.

Something hot and breathless tugged at his chest. A bullet brushed across his jacket. He brushed at it, as if it were a bug. Then he understood. *They're shoot-ing at you.*

He jerked up his knees, tucked his head between his shoulders. Why were they shooting at him? What had he done to them? He wasn't fighting anymore. Didn't they know he was helpless?

"I surrender," he yelled. "*Kamerad!*" Comrade. Friend. "*Kamerad, kamerad!*"

No, it wasn't fair. *Stop shooting.*

Ahead of him the first parachute had disappeared. Jack twisted around. Behind him Dave was frantically climbing up the side of his chute. They were shooting at him, too.

Why was it taking so long to reach the ground? Jack sensed the guns below aimed straight at him. He could feel the bullets rushing toward him. He was dropping too slowly. He'd never get down to the ground. They'd kill him first. He grabbed the ropes on one side of the chute and pulled them down. The canopy tipped, the air spilled out, and the chute collapsed. He dropped straight down, plunging toward the earth. He released the ropes and the canopy filled with air again.

Dave was above Jack now. Not moving, just hanging there, arms and legs straight down, head flopped for-ward. *He's playing dead so they won't shoot at him anymore.* He knew it was a lie.

The edge of the earth rose up all around him like a great shallow bowl. The ground was coming up at him. He saw trees, buildings, rooftops. He saw the shape of hills, and woods trailing down their sides.

He was a few hundred feet in the air, and drifting straight toward high-tension electric lines. He grabbed

the ropes on one side of the chute and dumped the
air. He fell down, straight down. High tension lines
... woods ... a stone cottage ... the ground rushing
up at him.

He released the shroud. The chute snapped up and
filled. He hit the ground. The balls of his feet felt
as if they'd been clubbed with hammers. His legs
collapsed. He fell forward. Something crunched under
his knees. The chute caught the wind and dragged
him forward.

He was on the ground. He was alive. Where were
the people shooting at him? His mind raced. The .45
was strapped under his arm. They'd killed Dave.
They'd killed Chuckie. They would kill him. He
glanced toward the stone cottage. He felt eyes watching him. He was shaking. He didn't know what to do
first.

The chute pulled him forward. He started hauling
it in. *To avoid detection by the enemy, bury your
chute at once.* He knelt, clawing at the ground. The
chute was still attached to his body. He fumbled with
the shackles, he couldn't make his fingers work. He
started digging into the ground again.

Shots like firecrackers popped all around him. They
were coming to kill him. He tore at the harness. His
hands trembled so violently they were useless. More
shots. Shots echoed up the side of the hill. It wouldn't
matter that he was ready to surrender, that he'd have
his hands up, calling *Kamerad.* They shot airmen and
strung them up on telephone poles.

He gathered the chute in his arms, pulled the yards
and yards of cloth up against his chest, and ran. The
chute kept falling under his feet, tripping him. He
went down in a heap, then came up. He ran, gasping,

stumbling over the chute. Down again, and up . . .
running . . . crouched low . . . running toward the
woods. They were going to kill him. Shots peppered
the air. He ran into the woods as fast as he could.

12

Jack fell to the ground. The chute billowed up around him. He stumbled up, dragging the tangle of silk and cords behind him, ran, fell over his big loose insulated boots, then ran again. He was in a panic, running. He had to hide, disappear. The world was crazy . . . out of control . . . everything was wrong.

One moment he'd been high in the air, safe in the airplane (in a minute they would have been turning toward home), and in the next moment they had been destroyed, Chuckie was dead, and he was falling through the air into a world where men with guns were trying to kill him.

He ran, searching for a place to hide, a safe place, the wild center of the woods, a hidden dark place where he could burrow and be silent. He ran between rows of trees laid out as evenly as the columns of a building. There was no underbrush. It was as if someone had swept the woods clean.

He ran straight down the hill, carrying the parachute in his arms. He was lost. He saw everything and nothing. He came to the end of the trees. An empty field lay before him. He crouched next to a stone fence, sucking air, his heart churning in his throat.

He felt everything—his feet, his ankles, his knees. Everything throbbed. The parachute was choking him, but he didn't let go. It was his, it had saved his life. Even if he could stop his hands from shaking long enough to release it, he wouldn't. He held it close to him like a bulky shield. It had softened every fall, he felt it would save him, it would even deflect bullets.

He went on. He came to a place where bushes and brambles grew together in a thick tangle over the wall. Unhesitatingly he threw himself under the brambles, squirmed his way into the thicket. He pulled the chute in behind him, wrapped himself in the silk, and pressed his face into the ground. The smells of earth and decaying leaves filled his nostrils.

He heard footfalls, felt the vibrations through his skin. *Kamerad*, he'd shout. He'd put up his hands. *Kamerad*. Then they'd shoot him, the way they'd shot Dave, or chop off his head, or hang him from a tree. He flattened himself against the ground. They'd see him. They'd see the white chute. He was lying there like an ostrich with his head in a hole.

He fumbled with the harness and finally loosened the shackles. He dug the chute into the ground, piled dead leaves and dirt over it. Above him on the hill he heard men shouting and more shots. He crept along the wall, flat on his belly, along the edge of the field. He heard a motor, then saw men with guns running across the field toward him.

He crawled on elbows and knees along the wall. He had to fight the desire to stand up and run for

his life. Through a break in the wall he saw a drain-
age ditch that ran along the other side. Carefully he
slid into the ditch and lay there, trying to guess which
way they were coming. He heard them whistling back
and forth. Shivers shot down his back. He wanted to
spring up and scream.

There were shouts. Police whistles. He crawled to
the edge of the ditch. There was no place for him to
go. He waited for them, shivering and listening. An
animal passing made his heart jump. His teeth chat-
tered. The shivering never stopped.

The voices receded, but he still lay there. He lay
in the ditch for a long time, weak with fear and grief.
*Chuckie was sitting crookedly across his seat, his feet
jammed under the table. Chuckie, the wing's shot off.
Chuckie. He pushed him. His head flopped forward.*

Jack started crying. Sobs shook him. He groaned
and wiped his mouth. Finally he lay still, drained.
His stomach ached from crying. He became aware of
the wind, blackbirds whistling in the trees. The men
were gone.

At dusk he found a sheltered place near some
bushes. He was sodden from the muddy ditch, soaked
to the skin. In a pocket of his coveralls he found his
emergency rations—crackers, cheese, and a square of
candy. He ate everything, then stripped, and wrung
out his clothes as best he could. He put his pants
back on, the wallet in his pocket, and then put his
shirt on inside out to hide the insignia. He made a
bundle of his flying helmet, flight coveralls, and
leather jacket with *Godfathers, Inc.* stenciled on it
and sank them all in the bottom of the ditch.

He put the gun in his pocket, but it stuck out. He

couldn't hide it. He sank the gun, as well. Carrying it was an invitation to be shot with no questions asked first.

The stars were coming out. A night wind stirred through the trees. He found the Big Dipper, then the North Star and using that as a guide began walking westward. West was the way back to the Allied lines.

He walked through fields along the edge of the woods. His feet slid around in the loose, fleece-lined flight boots. Blisters formed with every step. His ankles were wobbly and his knees ached where he'd fallen on them.

Before he ever saw it, he smelled the cottage, the sour smell of split wood. Then he heard the soft clucking of chickens coming from a coop behind the cottage. He was hungry. He'd grab a chicken, wring its neck, and run for the woods. He still had his lighter. He'd build a small fire and roast the chicken. The juices in his mouth flowed.

He circled the house cautiously. No lights. It was late. Everyone must be sleeping. He made out a wood pile, the gleam of an axe blade on a chopping block. Swallowing and swallowing he approached the chicken coop.

A dog barked, dry hollow sounds as loud as a man driving nails. Jack went down on his knees. The dog barked again and again. A man came out of the cottage and stood in the shadow of the house. Jack could just make him out. Silently, Jack backed away till he was on the far edge of the fields. Then he turned and ran back into the woods.

All night he moved slowly. His right knee became badly swollen. As the night wore on he became more and more indifferent to anything but his weariness, the burning scratches on his skin, the blisters on his feet, and his growing hunger.

Toward morning he found a place to hide in a deep ravine overgrown with high grass. He burrowed into the grass and fell asleep instantly.

When he woke it was broad daylight. He was tortured by thirst. His head was pounding. Every bone ached. In a wet spot at the edge of the grass he drank some brackish water. Then he slept again. He dozed all through the day. Dimly he heard voices, dogs barking, cows, the bleat of goats. Once, the unmistakable distant boom of heavy guns.

When he woke again the sun was casting long shadows across the hill above him. He was ravenous. He climbed, being careful to keep close to the brush. On the other side of the hill he saw a dirt road and a faded two-story wooden building with a porch around the upper floor.

He lay on the ground looking down at the house. There was an orchard near the house, trees in pink-and-white bloom. On one side of the house were a small barn and some sheds. A pile of broken machines lay against the barn. He waited and watched.

A girl wearing a man's coat went from the house to the barn carrying a pail. Then an older woman came out of the house with slops for the pigs. He saw no men and no dogs. Maybe he could talk to the girl. Tell her he'd work for them. Chop wood, fix things around the cottage, do chores. They were probably Czechs and hated Hitler, too. They'd tell him, Stay as long as you like, we'll hide you. He'd hide during the day and only come out at night.

The sun went down and still he waited, his stomach clenching with hunger. He felt he would do anything to get food.

Long after it was dark he crept toward the house. Inside a tool shed that smelled of hay and oil he found a bike and quietly wheeled it out. He circled the house till he found a low window next to the back steps. He forced the latch with a piece of metal. There was a sharp tinkle as something broke inside.

He waited, then pulled himself over the window-sill and inside. The warmth of the house, the smell of wool and cat, of milk and bread, made him suddenly so dizzy he had to squat till his head cleared.

The clock ticked heavily. The floor creaked. He was in an entryway next to the kitchen. Dark heavy clothing hung on pegs. There were boots on the floor.

He entered the kitchen. He smelled the milk. It was on the table in a covered earthenware bowl. He dipped his face into the liquid and drank it without stopping.

Against one wall was the dark warm bulk of a stove. He listened to the comfortable ticking of the clock. *Stay here*, it said to him. *Rest by the stove. You can get out in the morning before they wake up.*

A creaking noise made him turn. Somebody was coming down the stars. Jack stepped back toward the entry window. A man appeared in the doorway. An old man holding a club. He was breathing heavily.

Words of explanation crowded to Jack's lips. *I wasn't going to hurt anyone . . . I was so hungry . . . I'm sorry about breaking in . . .*

He took another step back. The old man didn't utter a word. "I'm sorry, sir," Jack whispered. He had one leg out the window when the old man, with a terrifying cry, came at him and struck him violently on the arm.

Jack fell back out of the window. The old man was shouting, rousing the house. Jack's arm hurt terribly. He thought it might be broken. With his good hand he got on the bike and pedaled wobblingly down the road.

He pedaled hard against the wind, expecting pursuit. The night had turned foggy and cold. Mist lay between the hills. He no longer knew which way he was going.

He pedaled through village after village. His arm throbbed. Only the barking dogs noticed him. He pedaled through all the dark hours. As the sky lightened he was weaving wearily from side to side. At dawn it began to drizzle.

Another cyclist overtook him, nodded, and said something. Startled, Jack looked up and nodded back. His heart pounded. He kept going. Nobody stopped him.

He walked the bike up a steep hill. His legs wobbled. He was exhausted. A group of girls came toward him. A tall girl with a blue beret cocked over one eye said something to him. No mistake, she was talking to him. Her friends giggled and stared at Jack. He told himself to smile, but he walked past her with his face frozen. They called after him, laughing.

He got on the bike again. He kept up a slow steady monotonous pace. It was easier to keep going than to stop and have to think about hiding. He entered the outskirts of a large town. Cyclists were on the road now, traveling in the same direction as Jack. The road curved down a hill. Brick factories lined one side.

He let the bike run free. He was bone weary, half asleep. Dimly he was aware of a little white structure ahead. The cyclists in front of Jack were slowing down, crowding together through an open gate. It was a checkpoint. Beyond it the road was open again.

Too late he saw the green uniformed soldier with the peaked cap. He stood with one foot up on a bench. A rifle lay on the bench.

Jack leaned back on the brakes, but he had gone too far. There was no place to turn off. The road led straight to the gate. He swung in behind a group of cyclists, keeping his head down. *Stay calm*. The cyclists were going through unchecked. The soldier hardly glanced at them. *Just ride through like everyone else*. But he was pumping too fast, his legs working independently of his mind. He bumped into the cyclist ahead of him. The man turned to look at him. "Sorry," Jack said. The English word rang in the air.

Jack kicked the pedal over and spun ahead, past the other cyclists, past the soldier, past the open gate. He turned and saw the soldier reach for his rifle. "Halt!"

Jack threw himself forward on the bike. There were no side streets, no turnoffs, just a long straight street that seemed to stretch for miles. A shot rang out. He felt it pass beneath his legs. His neck shriveled, his whole back felt skinned raw. He never heard the next shot, only felt the bike exploding under him.

13

Two German soldiers grabbed Jack before he had a chance to get to his feet. The bullet had grazed the inside of his thigh. His pants were torn. There was blood on his hands. The soldiers dragged him away from the road toward some low buildings. They jerked him forward across a railroad track, then threw him down in front of a brick wall.

The soldier with a burp gun clicked the safety off. The other, pale eyed, drew a big revolver from a long black holster. Everything in Jack went loose with fear. He waited for them to kill him. He expected to die. He kept blinking his eyes. He couldn't control it.

The pale-eyed soldier kicked him and made signs for him to take off his clothes. He had to sit up to pull off his boots. His hands were trembling. When the steam locomotive whistled, they'd put a bullet through his head and throw his body into a box car. He'd seen those pictures—Jews, Poles, Russians—stacks of naked bodies spilling from the cattle cars like animal carcasses.

The pale-eyed soldier tore the dog tags from Jack's neck and threw them on the ground with his wallet, handkerchief, and Zippo lighter. He sat there naked. Worse than naked. Without his dog tags his identity was gone, the proof that he was a soldier.

"American soldier," he said. He could say it in German. *Ich bin ein Amerikaner*. Or was that the Yiddish he'd picked up in his grandmother's house? He was afraid to say it. "American," he said again. He was stiff with fear. "American soldier."

The German with the burp gun started cursing. In that moment Jack thought of everyone he loved . . . his mother and father, Irv, Marcia . . . Good-bye . . . good-bye . . . my family, I love you all . . . Good-bye, Dotty.

The pale-eyed soldier poked at Jack's clothes with the tip of his boot. Behind Jack the German with the burp gun clicked the safety on and off, on and off. Jack stared blindly across the track, waiting . . . waiting.

His eyes teared. He pointed to the green army-issue handkerchief. He wanted that handkerchief. He wanted it very much, more than he ever wanted anything in his life.

The soldier kicked the handkerchief toward him. Jack looked up, looked at the soldier, then reached for the handkerchief. He wiped his face. He balled up the handkerchief and wiped his mouth.

Gesturing, the soldiers ordered him to dress again. Jack pulled on his pants and shirt. He didn't let go of the handkerchief. They weren't going to kill him, not yet, not here. When he stood up he was aware of everything. He felt the wind fresh against his face. He saw the long shadows cast by the brick wall, the shine of the rails, the holes dug into the mortar, and the red dust, like dried blood, at the foot of the wall.

The soldiers marched him along the railroad tracks, past factory buildings, then up a ramp to a railroad station. There were faces crowded at the windows, men and women, kids. They didn't speak. *"Links, rechts!"* Left, right. That was all. Would they shoot him with people around? No, not with women watching.

They followed a dirt road into the woods. The soldiers would kill him in the woods. There were trees on both sides of the road. There were long trenches along the road, some shaped like crosses. Every trench looked ready for a body. His body. One bullet and then they'd throw him into the trench.

The trees were laid out in even rows. He seemed to recognize them. This might have been where he buried the parachute. There was where he huddled against the stone wall. Everything was confused in his mind.

They came out of the woods. There was a highway and a sign with an arrow that read: PLZEN 7 KM. He was still in Czechoslovakia, hardly farther than when he'd started out. For two days he'd been going in circles.

There were houses along one side of the highway. On the other side was a chain fence topped with barbed wire. Through the fence he caught glimpses of swastikaed German fighter planes, hangars, and gutted buildings. They were on the edge of a military air base.

The soldiers marched him into the air base to a small block building. They left him in a bare room. There was a big wooden table, a filing cabinet. Above a narrow wooden bench hung a picture of Adolf Hitler. It seemed unreal, like the black swastika he'd seen on the German fighter planes. Two new guards stood at the door.

Jack sat on the bench for a long time. The inside of his leg burned where the bullet had grazed it. From time to time his eyes watered, and he wiped them with the green handkerchief.

A bald officer entered and stood looking at him. The guards at the door clicked their heels together. Jack stood up, his hands at his side. The German soldiers were like actors in a movie, with their shiny black-belted uniforms and their Heil Hitler salutes.

"I'm an American," Jack said. "American." He felt uncertain how he should act. He wanted to be brave. He didn't want the Germans to despise him.

The officer spread out the contents of Jack's wallet on the table. The English pounds, a picture of his parents, Dotty's last letter. He picked up Jack's dog tags, then put them down. He asked Jack questions in German, making motions with his hands. He wanted to know if Jack was a flyer, and where his plane came from. "England?" He made big flying motions with his hands.

Jack shook his head as if he didn't understand. *Act like a soldier.* He wasn't required to say anything except his name, rank, and serial number. "Staff Sergeant Jack Raab, 12-24-0202," he said. It was hard standing on his feet. He felt sick and dizzy. He hadn't eaten for a long time.

The officer repeated the same questions over and over, then suddenly stopped and examined Jack's dog tags intently. Jack's legs trembled. The "H" stamped on his dog tags stood for Hebrew. The officer would know he was a Jew. The Germans hated the Jews. They had killed so many already, what would one more mean?

The officer tossed the dog tags aside. "England?" he demanded again. "Staff Sergeant Jack Raab, 12-24-0202," Jack repeated. The officer called the guards. They stepped forward, heiled, then led Jack away. They took him to another building and locked him in a windowless cell.

He was alone. The darkness closed in on him. He felt his way along the length of the cell. There was straw along one wall. Four steps one way, two the other. He was alone, but alive. He ran his hand over the walls, felt things other prisoners had scratched into the stone. It was too dark to read.

He sank down on the floor. In the darkness he saw their plane, the wing chopped off like an amputated arm. He put his hand over his face, smelled coal and metal, the brassy smell of his guns . . . the radio compartment had been red with blood. . . .

"I'm Jack Raab," he said aloud. "I'm a soldier in the United States Army." He knocked on the wall. "Are you listening? My name is Jack Raab. I'm a soldier, a prisoner, an American, a Jew." He said it over and over. It gave him comfort. It made him feel better. He imagined someone was listening. He hoped someone was listening.

He lay down on the straw. It was damp and smelled of piss and mold. He wanted to sleep, but when he shut his eyes he saw Chuckie slumped at the table in the radio room . . . then Dave hanging from the shrouds. . . .

At last he slept fitfully. *He pushed Chuckie upright. . . . Come on, Chuckie, the wing's gone. . . . They were falling through the clouds. . . . Dave was playing dead. . . . The wing's gone, Chuckie! Come on, Chuckie. . . . Hurry! The old man's coming with a club. . . . Chuckie! Chuckie!* . . .

Before dawn, two guards roused him. They unlocked the cell door and motioned him out. *"Raus!"* Out. He was taken to a room where there were more guards. Weapons hung on the walls—rifles, clubs, and long leather straps. A large poster: *Blut ist recht.* Blood is right. They kept pushing him along.

They took him outside. It was dawn. They pushed him toward a small black bus standing by a gate. All the windows were painted black. A death bus. *"Geh schneller."* Faster! The guard gave him a shove, and he stumbled into the bus.

Hands pulled Jack down onto a seat. "What's up, doc?"

Jack's temples pounded. "You're American!"

"Charlie?" Someone cried. "Is that you, Charlie Matthew?"

"No. Jack Raab here."

A man groaned. "Get this bus moving! Take me to a hospital!"

There were eight other Americans on the bus. All flyers, all wounded. They lay on stretchers in the aisle, or sat bent over on the wooden benches. Jack went from seat to seat, searching each man's face. He could only see them dimly. "Who's here?" He tried to make out their faces. "Anyone here from the Three-Ninety-Eighth? Anyone here from *Godfathers*? Know anything about my crew? O'Brien, Johnson, Gonzalez, Eustice, White, Held, Seppetone, Martin. If you saw Chuckie O'Brien you wouldn't forget him. Guy with red hair, real Irish red hair."

No one said anything. There were groans and curses. Jack sat down. "Take it easy," the GI next to him said, but Jack couldn't stop.

"I think Chuckie's wounded. I don't know, maybe he's dead. I saw him in the plane before I bailed out. They shot us down over Pilsen." He was talking nonstop, everything was spilling out of him. "I ran, I hid in the woods, I hid for two days, then they got me."

The guy next to Jack handed him a cigarette. His head was bandaged. "My name is Stan Wakowski. We're all in the same boat. Nobody knows what happened to their crew. Your guys might be lucky. Look, you're here. They could be okay, too. You never know."

Jack took a deep drag on the cigarette. It went straight to his head. You never know. Maybe Chuckie had only been wounded and had bailed out after him. Maybe Dave really had been playing dead. Maybe they were all safe someplace. You never know. He tried to make himself believe it. Lieutenant Martin had landed the ship. Chuckie had been rushed to a hospital. Dave had been playing dead and come down okay. Paul was hiding out in the countryside right now.

Believe it, Jack told himself. He ordered himself to believe, but something at the bottom of his mind rejected everything. It had happened. He had seen it.

It had happened. It didn't matter what he said, what he told himself to believe. All the words, all the wishing in the world couldn't change it. . . . But, still, he hoped.

14

At nightfall the bus finally started. Groans rose from the wounded. They had had no food or water all day. Jack was supporting Pete, an aerial gunner who had ruined his hip when he bailed out. Pete hung on to Jack. He couldn't sit up or lie down. Every time the bus swayed he groaned.

There was a rotten smell in the bus. It was hot, stifling. All the windows were shut. Cries rose in the darkness. "Water. . . . Lord! . . . God. . . ." A cigarette was passed from man to man. Stan Wakowski passed it to Jack, who took a drag and then held the last puff to Pete's lips. Pete's forehead glistened with sweat.

The cigarette singed Jack's fingers. He dropped it. He was so tired. He felt as if he'd been holding Pete up forever.

"Water!" someone cried. "Water!" The cry was taken up. The men clamored and swore at the Germans, but the Germans heard nothing. The driver and the guards were in a separate compartment.

The bus kept stopping and starting and swinging around obstacles and falling into holes. After a while the clamor died down. Only the groans and the smell remained, and the feeling of helplessness.

Early in the morning, just after dawn, they arrived at a hospital in Klattau. The wounded were carried off the bus on stretchers by German medics. Jack, Stan, and an airman with a broken arm walked out. Stan Wakowski was dark. There was a bloodstained rag around his forehead and bruises on his face. Stan had been shot down over Pilsen the same day as Jack. He had bailed out and landed right where the bombs were exploding. Civilians had attacked him and nearly beaten him to death. German airmen, Luftwaffe men, saved him.

Jack put his hand up to his eyes. After the long hours on the bus, the light of day was blinding. He hobbled slowly. The bottom of his feet burned. A guard prodded him up the stairs into the hospital.

They entered a large marble-floored lobby. The severely wounded were taken away. Jack and Stan remained. There were wounded German soldiers everywhere, men in pajamas and red bathrobes. Jack stood stiffly. He didn't like being so close to the Germans.

"Where's the latrine?" he asked one of the wounded. The German looked at him from the corner of his eye and shifted his feet. "Latrine!" Jack repeated angrily. He hurt everywhere. He was exhausted, hungry, thirsty, and he needed a toilet.

"Latrine! Toilet! Water! *Wasser. Macht schnell. . . .*" Hurry up. He pointed to show what he meant.

"You tell them, Jack." Stan leaned wearily against a wall.

"Latrine," Jack said through his teeth. "You damned

Nazi, I'm dying!" He didn't give a damn about any
of them.

Finally a German medic took them downstairs. A
guard followed. Jack saw a fountain at the foot of the
stairs and started toward it.

"Halt!" the German guard ordered.

"Up yours." Jack didn't stop. He had to have a
drink. He was parched. He pushed his face into the
water, and drank and drank before stepping aside
for Stan.

They were taken to a toilet and then to the showers. With gestures and shoves they were told to shower.
Uneasily, Jack stripped, leaving his dirty clothes in
a pile. This was the way the Nazis killed the prisoners
in the concentration camps. Promised them showers,
but in the shower room it was poison gas that came
out of the showerheads.

Leaning against the tile wall, he let the hot water
run over him. The grayish bar of soap revolted him.
He couldn't touch it. The Germans had made soap
out of human fat, and lampshades out of human skin.

As he dressed, Jack became aware again of all the
wounded Germans around him. There was one man
with his foot gone at the ankle, another with phos-
phorus burns across his back. A big, blond blue-eyed
German, one of those perfect Aryan master-race types,
had a hole in his side where his hip should have been.

But even seeing them crippled, wounded, no longer
whole, Jack felt a chill. Hitler's master race. Forget
it, he told himself. There never was a master race,
just a lot of dumb clucks who swallowed Hitler's
garbage.

A German medic taped up the blisters on Jack's feet
and then took care of Stan. He had several deep cuts

on his head and some bad bruises where he'd been hit with rocks. Jack found he understood a great deal of what the Germans said. German was similar to Yiddish.

It was hard on him hearing German and remembering Yiddish. It left him feeling confused and lonely. Homesick, just plain sick for his home.

In a basement cafeteria Stan and Jack sat down at a long enameled table and were given gray potato soup and coarse black bread. Wounded German soldiers crowded around them. A legless soldier dug his wheelchair into Jack. Smiling, showing broken teeth, he offered Jack a cigarette.

Heat rose in Jack's throat. *"Nein."* He shoved away the cigarette. Friends already? Not for him. The war wasn't even over.

A German patted Stan on the shoulder. Another eagerly shook Stan's hand. It sickened Jack. He pushed away the remains of the soup. He didn't want to eat their food. He was tired and filled with disgust. Chuckie's blown-away head haunted him. He couldn't forget it, he'd never forget it.

Later that afternoon one of the nurses gave Jack a pair of old leather boots and a black wool sweater. She was young and wore glasses. She didn't look like a Nazi, but he couldn't help wondering where the boots had come from. In the stories and photos that had come out of the concentration camps he had seen the piles of clothes that had been taken from the ones who had been murdered.

Jack and Stan were locked into a windowless cellar room. There was a single light in the room. The black sweater was thick, but Jack couldn't stop shivering.

They passed a cigarette back and forth. "Where are

you from, Jack? I'm from Buffalo, New York. Know where that is?"

Jack nodded. "I'm from New York City—The Bronx. You ever been there?"

"Yeah, but I bet you've never been to Buffalo."

"How'd you know that?"

"Nobody goes to Buffalo. You haven't missed anything, Jack." He took the cigarette back.

"Chuckie was always bumming my butts," Jack said. He started going over the story of the way they'd been hit. He'd already told Stan two or three times.

"You know what I keep thinking?" he said to Stan. "Why did we have to fly? What was that mission over Pilsen all about? The war is as good as over." Jack was wound up like a spring, tense and argumentative. "Did it mean anything?"

Stan shrugged. "I leave that stuff to the generals. Forget it, Jack."

"You know what I can't forget," Jack said. "If we hadn't flown, Chuckie and all of them would be alive right now."

"You're going to drive yourself buggy thinking that way. What if? Who knows what if? If I hadn't volunteered for the Air Force, I could be sitting on my ass in London right now. Or, you and me, we could both be dead, as dead as all those poor bastards. Did you see those Germans in the showers? They got hit pretty bad, too."

"I hate the bastards," Jack broke in. "I hate all Germans."

"They're just doing what their government tells them to. They're just fuckin' unlucky in the kind of idiots they have running their country. That Hitler has to be a maniac." Stan shook his head. "The things he's done. Killing off people right and left. You see some of those stories in the papers about the Jews in the death camps? That place, Buchenwald?"

"I saw them." Jack held the butt gingerly and took a last puff. "Hitler didn't do that all alone, Stan. Some of those nice guys who were shaking your hand, maybe—"

Stan snubbed out the cigarette, then stripped the bit of paper and tobacco between his fingers. "I don't love the Jews, but I can't see knocking off people that way."

"That's big of you," Jack said.

"What are you getting hot about?"

"I'm a Jew, you dopey bastard!"

"Cool off. That doesn't surprise me. I thought so all along. You're from New York City. If you were from Buffalo I'd say ninety-nine chances out of a hundred you were a Wop or a Polack like me."

"You don't think any Jews live in Buffalo?" Jack said. "You think they all live in New York City?"

"I went to school with a couple of Jews," Stan said. "Harold Golden, and let's see—" He snapped his fingers. "Shirley Levine. Pretty girl, real pretty. How about you, Jack? You go to school with any Polacks?"

Jack had to laugh. "Sure, but I didn't call them Polacks. They would have knocked my teeth in. I called them Polish."

"It's okay with me," Stan said. "Let's shake on it."

Jack couldn't help liking Stan. It was hard to believe they'd only known each other two days. "Want to know something, Stan? How old do you think I am?"

"About the same as me, nineteen, maybe."

"Sixteen," Jack said. He'd always thought if he

ever told anyone, it would surely be Chuckie. And whenever he'd imagined it, it had been with an enormous sense of relief, of unburdening himself. "I'm sixteen," he said again. It was a flat statement of fact. "Three weeks ago, I had my birthday."

"You're bullshitting me," Stan said. "What're you doing in the Army?"

"I got in with my brother's birth certificate. They turned him down because of his heart. So I took it, and said it was mine."

"What'd you do that for?" Stan looked at him in amazement.

"I wanted to get Hitler. I had to do it."

"You mean being a Jew? Because of what Hitler did to your people?"

Jack nodded.

"I can see that," Stan said, "but I still think you're crazy. Volunteering to get killed, that's what you did. We're all going to die soon enough."

"You volunteered. Everyone in the Air Corps volunteers."

"I wanted those sergeant stripes and the flying pay. That's how stupid I was. Did your family want you to get in, Jack?"

"They don't know where I am. I just did it on my own."

"Hey, your poor mother," Stan said. "Sixteen? You dopey bastard! You should still be sucking lollipops."

15

Early in the morning the Germans roused them. In the distance they heard the thunder of a heavy artillery barrage. "Our guys," Stan said. "That's music to my ears. What do these krauts want now?" But there was no time for questions. Everything was "*Raus!*" Out!

Jack packed paper in the toes of the boots. They were a couple of sizes too big. He stood up, putting his weight gingerly on his feet.

Two new guards hurried them along. No time to wash, no time to eat. Jack, Stan, and the guards left the hospital. The other wounded American airmen were left behind. The German guards wore the blue uniforms of the Luftwaffe. They had rifles and rucksacks slung over their shoulders. The shorter one had pilot's wings with a swastika in the middle.

With the guards behind them, Jack and Stan were marched through the streets of Klattau. "Where the fuck are they taking us?" Stan said.

Jack had heard them talking. "We're going south."

"Why didn't they just leave us there?" Stan said. "The war's over. Don't they know it? They lost. It's just mopping-up time now."

Jack nodded. There was a weight on his chest. The war wasn't over, it was *almost* over. And they were still prisoners. Their German guards could do anything they wanted with Jack and Stan. They could march them into an alley, shoot them, and walk away. Who would know? Who would care?

Before they had gone more than a few blocks, the two guards loaded their rucksacks on Jack and Stan. People in the streets looked at them and asked the guards who they were. "*Amerikaner?*" a woman said. She spat at their feet.

A neatly dressed man wearing a hat and muffler knocked Jack's arm with his umbrella. "*Luftgangster!*" he exclaimed.

They left the town behind. On the highway bands of German soldiers were moving in the same direction. Panzer troopers in black leather uniforms, the gray-uniformed Wehrmacht, the regular army men, and the SS, Hitler's own troops, the worst Nazis of all. The SS had swastikas on their caps and tunics. Every time Jack saw the SS, everything in him tightened with fear and loathing.

They were all heading south. Willy and Karl, their guards, were talking about the Austrian Alps where Hitler had vowed to make a last stand. That was the direction they were moving in.

"Great," Stan said with feeling. "I suppose we're going there so we can fucking fight with him."

"*Ruhig!*" Shut up! The order came from Willy, the younger guard, the one with pilot wings. He was never still. He was short, quick, with a narrow alert face. He was a pilot without a plane—no petrol. Jack heard him complaining to Karl that the American bombers had seen to that.

Karl, the other guard, was older, easier, slower. He was supposed to be in charge, the ranking noncom, but it was Willy who did all the talking. Willy scouted out rides for them, mostly on military trucks where they packed into the back with a lot of grumbling German soldiers who didn't want the *"Verdammte Amerikaner"* with them. Jack preferred walking.

Everywhere they passed people on the move. On foot, on bicycles, with carts and wagons, carrying bundles and pillows and household goods, crowds of people, and all moving south, away from the Russian armies.

As they passed, people glanced at them with weary, expressionless faces that barely covered their hostility. Here and there someone was roused enough to curse the Americans, wave a fist, spit. Jack avoided their eyes and plodded on.

Late in the day they stopped near a one-room schoolhouse. Soldiers were bivouacked around the school. Willy went off, and Karl settled near Jack and Stan with his rifle across his knees. He took a loaf of black bread and a chunk of cheese from the rucksack. Jack couldn't bear watching Karl eat, and he couldn't tear his eyes away from the food.

Karl cut off a chunk of bread and tossed it to Stan. Stan divided it in half. Jack started to jam his piece into his mouth, then stopped and forced himself to take a small bite. He chewed it, then took another bite. His stomach clamored for more, but he put half his ration in his pocket for later.

Willy returned and drew them all together, indicating with gesture and sign and much repetition that he was about to tell them something of great importance. He gestured with his eyes to the black-clad SS soldiers, then shook his head.

"Schlecht. Schlecht!" The SS men were bad. Only they, the Luftwaffe, were in sympathy with the Americans. Jack kept translating for Stan. Willy made a sign for secrecy and whispered to Jack that soon, at the earliest opportunity, the four of them were going to go to the American lines.

"Alles kaput," Willy said. Everything is ruined. *"Der Krieg ist zu Ende."* The war is over. He handed Jack the remains of his cigarette. Jack took a puff and passed it to Stan. Willy gave them a wink. He was from Hamburg. It was in Allied hands. Soon, they would all go home.

"Ja," Karl solemnly agreed.

"Do you believe him?" Stan asked Jack later.

"I don't know. They want to surrender to the Americans because they're so scared of the Russians."

That night they slept under a table in the school-house. German soldiers kept entering the building throughout the night. Jack felt their boots on the floor and couldn't sleep. He'd doze off and then wake with his heart pounding. It was his old nightmare of the Nazis coming to their house. Leather creaked, metal struck metal. For a long time he couldn't get back to sleep.

16

For five days they were on the road. Jack's feet were blistered worse than ever. He dug bread crumbs from his pocket. The gnawing feeling in his stomach never left him. Karl supplied them with half a German soldier's ration that Jack and Stan divided between them.

Willy kept promising to take them to the American lines, but all they seemed to be doing was walking . . . walking . . . walking. . . . Was Willy lying to them? He kept repeating that they were going to surrender to the Americans. Maybe he was just saying that for insurance. Then if they ran into the Americans he and Karl would have Jack and Stan to speak up for them. The longer they went on, the less Jack believed Willy. It felt sometimes as if this walking would go on forever.

There were kids everywhere on the road, gangs of kids, boys and girls. Kids on crutches, kids begging, skinny, ragged kids. Once Jack saw two girls pulling a legless boy in a wooden wagon.

All those bombs they had dropped—he had never thought they would be blowing kids away. He'd always thought they were bombing war factories and seaports. Military targets. Oil dumps, rail terminals. But they'd hit a lot more than that. Along some of the rail lines they passed he saw whole towns that were obliterated.

On the afternoon of the sixth day they climbed up into sandy hills, past pine woods, past crowds of refugees, past tank traps set like wooden teeth in the road. In a village Willy knocked on a door to ask for water. In the streets chickens picked in the dirt. Jack sank down in the shade of a building. Stan collapsed next to him. Karl seated himself nearby. He never moved when he didn't have to.

At the door of the cottage Willy was talking to a woman. Finally she brought out a pot of coffee and milk, and then shut the door. Willy and Karl filled their tins and passed what was left in the pot to Jack and Stan. It wasn't real coffee; it was more like warm, coffee-flavored milk.

They started off again, traveling through tracts of forest. Passing vehicles covered them with dust. Jack smelled the pines, heard birds call. At times he dreamed he was home in Bronx Park, walking through the woods.

As the afternoon wore on the sky clouded, the air turned damp and cold. Rain threatened. At dusk, just as it began to drizzle, they came to a railroad station. They huddled outside, then boarded a crowded train that carried them further south into the mountains. Jack slept sitting upright in the corridor.

Freight cars rolled by. He heard the knock of the wheels. In the mist and the smoke he began to imagine that the freight cars were packed with people being transported to concentration camps. He could almost hear the shuffle of fists against wooden walls, the cries for water, the cries for help that never came. For a moment he imagined himself on that sealed train, a Jew among Jews, packed in so tightly he could neither move nor breathe.

It's a nightmare . . . stop thinking about it. . . . Yes, for him it was a nightmare, but it was happening. Somewhere there were people screaming . . . they would scream on into eternity.

In the morning they left the train and began walking again. In a village a priest gave Jack and Stan each a hardboiled egg. A real egg. Jack held the egg in his hand just looking at it. It was oval and brown and smooth. He put it carefully in his pocket savoring the thought of eating it. Not now, not while they were walking. He'd eat it later when they stopped, taking his time and making the egg last as long as possible.

They were in a land of mountains. They passed through tiny villages full of small whitewashed houses with straw roofs. Here there were no signs of war. Roosters crowed, dogs barked, children played in the streets. He smelled straw and burning wood. He walked without thinking, smelling the air, rolling the egg between his fingers.

At noon they stopped by a military station. Jack sat by the side of the road. He peeled the egg slowly, enjoying flaking off the shell. Stan looked at him and laughed. He had eaten his egg when the priest gave it to him.

Jack was just about to take a bite of the egg when

he saw someone watching him. It was an eight- or nine-year-old boy wearing a man's ragged gray sweater and a German forage cap with the brim pulled up. He squatted down opposite Jack, his eyes on the egg, his grimy face tucked between bony knees. There were kids like him all over the place. "Scram," Jack said. He started to take a bite, but he couldn't eat his egg with the kid watching him.

Stan threw the boy a piece of bread. He caught it and swallowed it fast. He came closer, close enough for Jack to smell him. He was rank. Jack stared at him. Who was he? Some little Jew hater who'd swallowed Hitler's crap with his baby food?

The kid eyed the egg, then Jack, then held out his hand. *"Nein,"* Jack said. He could almost taste the egg crumbling deliciously in his mouth. It was his egg. "I'm not giving this to some little Nazi."

Twice Jack started to bring the egg to his mouth, and twice he stopped. A little Nazi? Or a little Jewish kid? He had that same big-eyed, starving look the survivors in the death camps had. Jack swore under his breath. He'd never know. Maybe the boy wasn't a Nazi, or a Jew, but just another hungry kid. "God-damn it!" He held the egg out. He was going to share it, but the boy grabbed it from him and swallowed it whole. He almost choked getting it down.

When the boy had cleaned the last bits of yolk off his teeth, he produced a little sack of tobacco from inside his filthy sweater. He rolled a cigarette, twisted it at both ends, lit it, took a puff, then with a little flourish handed it to Jack.

"He's paying you back for the egg," Stan said.

"Big shot," Jack said. It was the first time he'd smiled in days.

17

Jack, Stan, and the two guards crossed the Danube River over a long makeshift railroad bridge into Austria. Suddenly they were caught in a war zone. On both sides of the road camouflaged trucks and tanks were hidden under trees and against the sides of buildings. They passed burned-out trucks, and dead bloated horses lying on their backs. Sections of road were blown away. They had to detour constantly. They passed roofless houses. There was rubble everywhere.

"Macht schnell." Willy urged them to go faster. He and Karl kept looking up, on the alert for strafing Russian and American fighter planes. Jack watched the skies, too. Bullets wouldn't know the difference between Germans guards and American prisoners.

They got a ride on a German halftrack troop carrier. Willy talked the commander into taking them along. They climbed in the back. A spotter sat on top of the cab looking out for enemy planes.

A young soldier with a swastika buckle on his belt turned to Jack and Stan. *"Alles kaput,"* he said. All is over. Hitler was dead. He'd heard it on the radio.

There had been a time when Jack had thought that Hitler's death would solve everything. End the destruction, the pain, the war. Now he was dead. Dead at last! Jack thought, fiercely glad. But they were still prisoners. Chuckie was still dead. It was all still going on. The soldier smiled at Jack and Stan. He wanted them to know he liked Americans. The war would soon be over. The Americans and the Germans were going to be friends now. They should never have fought against each other.

Germans have culture, he said. Refinement. The Jews had made the war. The Germans and the Americans fought each other, and the Jews got fat. *"Verdammte Juden."*

Heat rose to Jack's face. "Son of a bitch," he said to Stan. "Stupid bastard!"

They rolled out from under a canopy of trees. There was a shout from the spotter on top of the cab. *"Jäger!"* Fighter! The troop carrier jolted to a halt. Men dove in every direction. Jack flung himself off the truck and ran for a ditch. A shadow swept overhead, a dark shape over the trees. There was a roar and a sudden hammering. The leaves in the trees shredded. Dust spit up in the road.

In seconds the plane was gone. Jack climbed out of the ditch. "Stan?" He was afraid. Then Stan crawled out from under the truck. "Jack. You okay?" Jack nodded. His heart was still thudding. One man lay on the ground. A soldier bent over him. A wet patch spread beneath the dead man's body. It was the young German with the swastika belt.

He was lifted onto the truck, his coat thrown over his face. Everyone climbed back on. Jack hung on to the side of the carrier. Space was left around the corpse. Once or twice Jack looked over to where the dead man was lying. There were identical holes worn in the soles of his boots. Jack felt the hatred drain from him. In death the man had stopped being a German, a Jew hater, a Nazi, or anything at all—except a dead man.

May sixth, their seventh day on the road, Willy and Karl led them into a Wehrmacht camp in the Austrian Alps. They were in a broad valley ringed with mountains. The camp, a regular German army camp, was surrounded by a barbed-wire fence. At first Willy said they were stopping only for food. Then in the corridor of the headquarters building he suddenly told them he and Karl were going back to Germany and wanted to leave Stan and Jack here. The Russians were nearby, on the Enns River, and they were afraid.

"What about the Americans?" Jack asked in his rough German. "I thought we were going to the American lines together."

"*Schweig!*" Quiet! Willy said. It was too late for that. Then he hurried off to find the Commandant. In a few moments he came back with a tall, stiff-backed man who walked with a cane. The Commandant looked over Stan and Jack and asked them where they were from.

"*Amerikaner,*" Jack answered. He was worried. The Commandant was a cold, stiff-looking German. He didn't know what to expect.

The Commandant turned to Willy and Karl and dismissed them. Willy snapped to attention, heiled

Hitler, and he and Karl left without a word to Jack and Stan.

Two new guards appeared and led them to another building where they were locked in. "Here we go again," Stan said.

They were in an empty classroom. On the walls over the blackboard were charts showing parts of quartered animals. In one corner was a pile of straw. A guard remained outside the locked door, and the other guard was at the window.

Stan fell down in the straw. "Old Willy and Karl were sure eager to get rid of us."

"Who cares?" Jack said. "As long as they feed us." He was trying to put the best face on it, but he was alarmed. At least with Willy and Karl they knew where they stood—or thought they did. He sat down on the floor next to Stan and pulled off his boots. He couldn't keep his head from jerking around at every loud noise.

Nobody brought them food. They went to sleep hungry. Later, around midnight, Jack woke to the sharp bark of gunfire. In the corridor he heard the Germans talking excitedly.

"*Russen. . . . Russen. . . . Russen kommen!*" The Russians are coming!

The Russians were coming. The Germans were running from them. Maybe the Russians were here already. They might be free right now, Jack thought, and not even know it. He couldn't sleep. He listened and listened, peering into the darkness, but no one came.

In the morning there were no guards at the door or the window. The door was still locked, so they climbed out the window. Jack dropped to the ground,

followed by Stan. Cautiously they crept to the edge
of the building. Everywhere they looked German soldiers carrying sacks and bundles were running this
way and that. Nobody paid any attention to Jack and
Stan.

Jack grabbed a passing German. *"Was ist
geschehen?"* What's happening?

"Der Krieg ist zu Ende!" The German ran on.

Jack and Stan looked at each other. "The war's
over!" They embraced, pounded each other on the
back. Stan let out a yell. "Whoopeeee!" Then Jack
jumped on Stan's back. "I don't believe it! Is it really
over! Hey, the war's over," he shouted.

Stan staggered around, bouncing Jack up and down
and yelling.

Stan stopped a German and pointed to his holstered
revolver. The soldier removed it and handed it to him.
"Jesus!" Jack said. He looked around for a gun and
got a Luger from another soldier. It was as easy as
that.

The Germans were ready to give them all their
guns. They could have had pistols on both hips and
rifles slung over their shoulders. They were free. It
was true. The war was really over. They strapped the
guns to their waists, then looked around for a way
out.

In a motor pool full of abandoned vehicles they
found a black Volkswagen. A couple of tires had to
be changed. Jack took two tires from another VW,
while Stan fooled with the carburetor and got the car
started.

They drove through the camp. Cars and trucks
loaded with Germans were lined up at the gate. They
were being checked by the guards. "Let's go, let's go,"

Jack said. Was the war really over? Were they really free?

The guard peered into the car. *"Amerikaner!"* Jack said boldly. *"Amerikaner."* The guard waved them out of line and through the gates. *Amerikaner* was the magic word. As they went through the gates, Stan leaned on the horn.

"Amerikaner! Amerikaner!" Jack yelled, and the Germans gave way, opening a path for them.

German soldiers fleeing the advancing Russians clogged the road by the thousands, spilling into the field, moving toward the American lines. Arms and weapons filled the ditches. Every house they passed carried the flag of surrender: a white sheet dangling from a window.

"Raus!" Jack screamed at the Germans. "Get the hell out of our way."

"Tell 'em, Jack! Tell 'em, Jack," Stan screamed. They were crazy. They were the Americans.

"The war's over," they screamed.

Hitler was dead in Berlin. The master race had gone down the drain. *When the Führer says we are the master race, we heil—splaat!—heil—splaaat!—right in the Führer's face!*

Chuckie. . . . Oh, Chuckie . . . it's all over. . . .

For a long time they didn't see anyone but Germans. No Russians, no Americans. They drove into the hills, west, toward the American lines, leaving the Germans behind them in the valley.

Ahead, an American Sherman tank blocked the road, its long muzzle pointed straight at them. Stan stopped the car. Armed American GI's surrounded them. Jack poked his head out of the window, grinning.

"Out of that car, kraut," a soldier said. The soldiers pulled open the doors and yanked them out.

"You idiots, we're Americans."

The soldiers looked at them disbelievingly. Jack and Stan had come from the German lines in a German car. They were unshaven, dirty, wearing German boots and carrying German guns.

"Say that again," a GI demanded.

"We were POW's," Jack said.

"I'm from Buffalo, New York," Stan said.

"I'm from The Bronx. Can't you tell by the way I talk?"

"You want us to sing the 'Star Spangled Banner'?" Stan stood at attention. "Oooh, say can you seee—"

Suddenly hands were grabbing them. "Americans, huh? Waddya know. Well, welcome home!"

PART IV

HOME

At the end of a war there are three armies. The army of the wounded, the army of the dead, and the army of the mourners.

From a German proverb

18

Jack and Stan said good-bye at the military airport in Munich. It was less than a week since they had joined up with the American forces. Now Stan was going to Paris, while Jack was going to Camp Lucky Strike near Rouen, a gathering point for ex-POW's, to see what he could find out about his crew.

A ragged German beggar was picking up American cigarette butts from the ground. "Hey—" Stan handed the man a cigarette. The German nodded and bowed and thanked him profusely.

Jack turned away and walked toward the plane. Once, years ago it seemed, but it had only been months before, the thought of a German humiliated would have filled him with satisfaction. Now, he didn't know, he just didn't know. Nearly anything could make him feel sick, or disgusted, or angry.

Traveling to Munich, he had seen the German countryside bombed flat. The center of Munich was nothing but mud and rubble covered with makeshift roads and wooden walks. There were places where it was impossible to believe anything had ever stood. Impossible to believe people had lived and worked there. Even the bricks had been ground into sand.

It was the war, Jack kept reminding himself, the war the Germans had brought on themselves.

"Listen, Buddy—" Stan caught up with him. "Stay in touch. You got my address?"

"Right here." Jack touched his breast pocket.

"You're coming to Buffalo."

"And you're coming to The Bronx."

Stan stuck out his hand. "Well, we made it, anyway, Jack. That's saying something."

They shook hands. A wave of emotion hit Jack. He grabbed Stan around the neck.

Afterwards in the plane, a big cargo-carrying DC-3, he looked out a window and waved. Stan threw his cap in the air. When the plane took off Jack sat on a pile of duffel bags. He was tense. Couldn't control it. That old feeling, his stomach knotting, as if they'd never get off the ground. But worse this time. It was the first time since Pilsen he'd been in a plane. It was a short flight, but he was in a sweat when he got out of the plane.

The first thing Jack did at Camp Lucky Strike was to go to the Red Cross telegraph office and send a telegram home. He had to keep it to ten words. "IM OK STOP COMING HOME SOON STOP LOVE YOU ALL MOM ESPECIALLY STOP (SIGNED) S/SGT IRVING JACK RAAB."

After he sent it he hung around the office for a while listening to the tick of the typing machines. The clerk said it would take a week to deliver his message, but in Jack's mind it was there already. Just writing out the address—2600 Bronx Park East, Apt.

4E—had made him homesick. He could see them reading the telegram right now. They'd all be sitting in the kitchen alcove in front of the window. His mother would read the telegram out loud. His father would be pacing the floor, smoking and looking up at the ceiling. Marcia would notice Jack's signature. "Jack's a sergeant! He's in the Army!" And Irv would figure out everything, how Jack had gotten in and where he'd been this whole year.

Camp Lucky Strike was a huge tent city where the Army was processing, checking, and reassigning all the newly freed American POW's. In the next few days while he waited for his traveling orders, Jack studied every roster in every office in the camp, looking for news of his crew. He spent days searching for a familiar face. Once he saw an officer with shoulders like Milt Held. Another time he heard a slow soft Carolina drawl like Billy's. But it was never them.

A lot of the POW's were in bad shape, their hair falling out from lack of food, their teeth rotting.

Everything bothered Jack. Not finding out anything about his crew . . . all these battered GI's. One ex-POW he got to know shook so badly he couldn't talk without hanging on to something solid.

At the end of a week Jack's traveling orders came through and he flew back to his old base on a B-17. He swung up into the plane through the head-end hatch, into the navigator's compartment. He didn't go back to his old position.

The flight wasn't as bad for him as the flight from Munich. He watched the water beneath him, the chalk-white coast of England, and the bright green land beyond. They came down at Northumberland. Jack went immediately to 602nd Squadron Headquarters. He felt sure they would know the fate of his crew.

As he neared Squadron Headquarters, his step slowed. It was going to be settled now, once and for all. He was almost afraid to enter the squad room. Wolpe, the clerk who used to wake them in the morning, was sitting at a desk, typing.

"Raab." Wolpe stared at him. "What the hell are you doing here? Sergeant!" He called the master sergeant. "Look who's here. Raab from Martin's crew." They both stared at him. "We thought you were dead," Wolpe said.

Then Jack knew it was going to be bad, as bad as it could be.

Wolpe got the crew reports from the files. "Aircraft piloted by Lieutenant G. Martin seen to have been hit in left wing by flak," Wolpe read off. "Smoke reported coming from number two and number three engines. Aircraft seen to do several violent spins. Went down through clouds in steep dive. No survivors observed."

"Didn't they see the parachutes?" Jack said. "There were three chutes, for Christ's sake!"

"No one saw any chutes."

"There were three chutes," Jack repeated. "Dave Gonzalez, Paul Johnson, and me."

"Look," Wolpe said, holding up a sheaf of pink papers, "this came in from Army Intelligence two days ago. It's about your crew." He paused. "They found the plane. Six bodies buried in a common grave. Six bodies, positive identification from dog tags. Martin, Held, Seppetone," he read. "Pratt, Eustice, O'Brien. And there's another report here on

Johnson and Gonzalez. They were both shot and
killed. You were the only one not accounted for. I'm
sorry, sergeant," he added. "It's rough losing your
whole crew."

Jack was afraid to speak. He walked out, senselessly
angry with Wolpe. *Fuckin' squad-room commandos,
fighting the war on their asses . . . talk, that's all they
know how to do . . . talk, and read reports . . . words
. . . words . . . just a lot of fuckin' words. . . .*

Outside he grabbed a bike leaning against the building and headed toward their Nissen hut. He pedaled
with his head down. The sun beat on his back. Listening to Wolpe it had all come back afresh. Chuckie in
the radio room, Dave climbing up the side of his
chute. . . .

The Nissen hut seemed smaller. It looked rusted
and half sunk into the ground. He pushed open the
door. Inside it was cold, and smelled of earth and
coal dust. Everything was gone. The room was bare.
Their beds stripped, lockers emptied.

His old locker door was jammed open. A pair of
pants stretchers were caught in the door. He found an
unopened pack of Lucky Strikes in back of the shelf,
and some cellophane-wrapped Lorna Doones the mice
had gotten into. His pictures were still tacked up on
the door.

He took down the photo of Dotty, and the one of
Chuckie and himself that Dave had taken the time
they were all digging ditches. There they were,
Chuckie and Jack, with their arms around each other,
grinning out at the world.

He looked around, touched the stove, ran his hands
over the rusting surface. Then he sat down on a

wooden box, hunched over, elbows on his knees. He sat there as if he were waiting for something . . . waiting for the others to return.

He concentrated on the stove, its roughness, the wet cinder smell. Go, he told himself, but he couldn't leave. *You're alive, they're dead. Go.* He glanced at the door standing ajar, the stripe of blue sky. He wished he could hear one of those rousing Army songs that used to set his feet marching, his chest thrown out, his head high.

Off we go into the wild blue yonder, flying high into the sun. . . .

So proud to be up there in the clouds, to be an airman, to be in the war.

He listened. There was a buzz of insects from outside, like a distant plane. Wind rippled along the metal skin of the hut. All those beautiful lies about soldiers, and war, and boys in battle.

He put his hands over his face. Chuckie . . . Billy . . . Dave . . . oh, God, oh, God. . . .

19

Jack crossed the Atlantic on an LST. The LST's were floating washtubs with big doors that opened in front. The Navy had used them to carry invasion troops right up onto the beaches of France. It was a small ship. Apart from the crew and a group of Dutch marines going to the States for training, there was hardly anyone else on board. That suited Jack fine. He played cards, slept a lot, and stood on the ship's fantail watching the gulls swoop for the garbage.

It took them nearly two weeks to cross. They landed at Newport News, Virginia. The whole crew and all the Dutch marines were on deck, everyone straining to be the first to see land. It was sunset when they saw the coast. The sea and the ship were bathed in a golden light. He remained on deck as they approached the harbor.

Night fell. The lights of the city and the ships they passed thrilled him. Land, home, country . . . his country.

* * *

"Hello?" Jack said. "Hello!" He heard the phone ringing. He had butterflies in his stomach. The phone rang twice, three times. Whoever answered would have to buzz his family's apartment for someone to come down.

"Hello?" a woman said. "Who do you want?"

"Raab," Jack said. "Apartment four E. Will you ring them? This is long distance."

Then he had to wait again. He looked at his pile of coins. Why was it taking so long?

"Hello." It was his sister, Marcia.

"Marcia?"

"Yes, this is Marcia. Who is this?"

"Your brother."

"Jack?" she said.

"Yes." He started crying.

"Jack," she screamed. "Where are you?"

"I'm home. In the United States. I'm in Virginia, and—"

"Jack, are you coming home? Jack, let me get Mom."

"Wait, Marcia, is everyone all right? Did you get my telegram?" He didn't want her to go. He was afraid the connection would be broken.

"Let me get Mom," she said again. She dropped the phone. He could hear it banging against the wall, and Marcia galloping up the stairs screaming at the top of her lungs. "Mom! It's Jack, it's Jack. . . . Mom!"

He stacked and restacked his coins. He could hear them coming down the stairs, their voices distant and hollow. Shivers ran down his back.

"Jack—" His mother's deep familiar voice came over the phone. "Jack, my darling. . . ."

They hardly talked. They were both crying. "I'm coming home, Mom," he kept saying. "I'm coming home."

The war against Japan was still going on. Soldiers like Jack were being sent as replacements to the Asian war theater. It wasn't going to be easy getting out of the Army. A point system was used for early discharge, favoring combat veterans with long overseas service. Jack didn't have half enough points.

There was one clear way for him to get out of the Army, and that was to tell them how old he was. But he delayed. He was afraid it would be bad for him unless they had his overseas records. They didn't have them yet at Newport. That was what kept holding up things.

Day after day he was kept waiting. "Sorry, sergeant," the clerk said, glancing at Jack's gunner wings. Under the wings Jack wore all his ribbons—the ETO ribbon, the Air Medal with the three Oak Leaf Clusters for flying twenty-five missions, and the Purple Heart they'd given him.

He showed up at the office every day, and every day it was the same thing. "We're processing your papers, sergeant, come back this afternoon. . . ." Or, "Come back tomorrow. . . ."

Jack read, or shot pool in the noncom rec room. Killing time. Going through the motions of living, while hour by hour he felt that real living was only at home, with his family, the streets he'd known all his life, old friends . . . his longing for all that was intense and unending.

He called home almost every day and even wrote a couple letters. He wrote Dotty, as well, but he didn't call her. He didn't feel ready yet to speak to her. He was working up his nerve to tell her the truth about his age.

More than once after hearing "Come back tomorrow, sergeant," he thought of just forgetting the papers and the processing, and hitching a ride home. But he worried that if he went AWOL it would hurt his chances of getting out. He was in the Army until he was out of the Army, and that meant he was the Army's man until the Army released him.

After a week he was sent to the Air Corps Distribution Center at Atlantic City, New Jersey. More delay. Now he was so close to home he could almost taste that hot New York City air.

Atlantic City was like Miami Beach had been when he was doing basic training. All the big hotels along the ocean had been taken over by the Army. The boardwalk was crowded with airmen. Jack was assigned a room and a place to eat. And then the lines and the questions and the checkups began again.

On his second day in Atlantic City Jack saw a clerk who was processing his papers scribble something about B-29 School. B-29's were bigger bombers than the B-17's and were being used against the Japanese. They were going to send him to school somewhere out west, and then to the Asian Theater. Jack's heart dropped.

That night when he called home he spoke to his father. "Pop, they're not going to let me out. They're assigning me to B-29's."

"How can they keep you?" his father said reasonably. "Don't they know how old you are? I thought you told them."

"I didn't tell yet, Pop." Just talking to his father

calmed Jack. "They don't have my overseas records."

"You tell them how old you are, Jack. You want me to come down there? I'll talk to the Army for you. I'll tell them."

Jack could just imagine his parents in Atlantic City talking to the officers about their son!

"Stay home, Pop! I don't want you to come." Then he apologized because that sounded so rough. "I don't mean that the wrong way. I want to see you and Mom, but at home. Not here."

"You sure, Yankele?" his father said, using the Yiddish diminutive of Jack's name. Little Jack.

Jack started laughing. "Pop, I'm a staff sergeant, I've been in combat, flown twenty-five missions, I've been a prisoner of war—"

"Okay, okay," his father said, a little huffily, "I get the picture. You're a big man now."

"I'll take care of it, Pop. Tell Mom I love her, and you, too." He hung up fast.

Then and there he went to the service center to the corporal who'd been handling his papers. "Corporal, I have something to tell you. I'm sixteen. My name isn't Irving Raab, it's Jack Raab, and I got into the Air Force using my brother's papers."

The corporal just looked at Jack for a moment. Then he got the lieutenant.

"How old did you say you are?" Lieutenant Spaid asked.

"Sixteen, sir." Jack stood with his hands clasped behind his back, his overseas cap tucked neatly into his belt, while the lieutenant went over his papers.

"Sergeant, it says right here that you were born in nineteen twenty-six. That would make you nineteen." The lieutenant had a high smooth forehead.

"That's not right, sir. That's my brother's birthday. I used his records to get into the Air Corps."

The lieutenant touched his forehead. "Why?"

"I did it because I wanted to serve my country, sir."

"And now you want to get out of the Army, sergeant?"

"Yes, sir."

Lt. Spaid looked at Jack. "This is all very unusual,
sergeant. There will have to be an investigation to
straighten out this mess."

Until the "mess" could be straightened out, Jack
was kept in the guardhouse. He was not allowed to
call home. He was not allowed to write letters. He
was treated as if he were, at the very least, an enemy
spy. He was interrogated three times, twice by Lieutenant Spaid, the third time by a Major Barth.

"How old were you when you entered the Air Corps,
sergeant?" Major Barth said.

"My real age, or my false age, sir?" Jack said. It
was at least the fifth time he'd answered the question.

"You claim that you are Jack Raab?"

"No, sir, I don't claim. I *am* Jack Raab. Irving
is my brother. I was fifteen when I volunteered. Do
you have my overseas records—"

"Let me ask the questions, sergeant." Major Barth
looked tired.

"Yes, sir."

"Now, the papers you used—"

"My brother's, sir. He knew nothing about it."

More questions. The same questions he'd answered
before. Major Barth concluded the interrogation without giving Jack any indication of whether he believed
him or not.

Ten days after he was put in the guardhouse, Jack

was called before a room full of officers sitting behind
a table. Major Barth and Lieutenant Spaid were both
there.

"At ease, sergeant." He stood at parade rest. His
clasped hands behind his back were icy.

The officers questioned him closely, once again
taking him over all the details of his enlistment and
service. They asked about his crew, and the missions
he'd flown. "Did anyone on your crew know your real
age, sergeant?"

"No, sir. I was going to tell my best friend, but I
never did."

"Why not, sergeant?"

"I was afraid to, sir. I didn't want to be thrown
out of the Army."

They went over everything. Question after question. All the missions he'd flown, the bail out, being
captured, right to the moment he was liberated.

The officers shuffled papers and passed them back
and forth down the long table. They had Jack's overseas Army service and records. "One more question,
sergeant." It was Lieutenant Spaid. He passed his
hand over his forehead. "Why did you decide to tell
the truth about your age now?"

"I'm sixteen, sir. I haven't seen my family in over
a year." He cleared his throat. "And Hitler is dead."
He stopped. There was nothing else to say.

"I think it's clear to all of us," Major Barth said
in his weary voice, "that this soldier has served
honorably and well. He took part in the last Eighth
Air Force mission in the European Theater. He had
the difficult and tragic experience of being the only
survivor of his crew. The real question is his age. Are
we all satisfied that Sergeant Raab is, in fact, sixteen,

as he claims, and not nineteen as the official record states?"

One by one the officers nodded their heads. Major Barth said, "I think, then, we can recommend an immediate discharge."

A grin spread over Jack's face, an uncontrollable smile. "Thank you, sir!"

Major Barth stood up. "I don't think it's a laughing matter, sergeant, to lie to the United States Army!"

Jack struggled with his smile. "Sorry, sir."

"You may think you were very clever putting something over on the United States Army, but believe me the Army doesn't regard it as funny. The rules are there for a reason and the Army doesn't smile on anyone who breaks those rules, no matter how good their reasons may be. Do you understand, sergeant?"

"Yes, sir." Jack stood at attention, his face blank but his heart throbbing.

"We're not happy with what you've done, sergeant. Do you know we could have recommended a general court-martial?"

"Yes, sir!" Even after Jack heard the major order an immediate discharge he continued to stand at attention, his face expressionless. It was only after he was dismissed and out of the room that he let himself breathe again.

20

One evening several days later, Jack, a B-4 bag on his shoulder, climbed the four flights of stairs to his family's apartment. He flew up the last flight and rang the bell. He was grinning, and his heart was pounding.

"Who's there?" It was his mother's voice.

"Mom, it's me!"

The door opened. He saw his mother, tall, her faded green robe, her hair in a long loose braid down her back.

"Yankel!" Her fingers dug into his skin. She held his head and kissed him repeatedly.

His father came running and gave Jack a tremendous blow on the back. Then Marcia, in her long nightgown. "Jackie! My brother Jackie!" She got her arms around his waist and hung on. And finally, Irv, reaching around the others to shake Jack's hand. "How are you, brother?"

They went into the living room and Jack sat on

the old red plush couch between Marcia and his mother. "What did they do to your hair?" His mother brushed her hand over his GI cut. "They shaved your head and you had such beautiful hair." She laughed. "What do I care about your hair? Your hair will grow."

Irv stood by the window, his arms folded. "You lost weight," he said. "Don't they feed you anything in the Army?"

"We thought you were dead," Marcia said. "We got the telegram—missing in action."

"How'd you know it was me?"

"We knew," his father said, nodding his head. "When that telegram came, we knew."

"I didn't believe it," his mother said. "I never for one minute believed you were dead." She stroked his arm.

"What happened when your plane got hit?" Marcia said. He had told her on the phone, and written about it, but she wanted to hear everything again, and right away.

"You jumped out of the plane? How'd you do it, Jack? My brother! The Germans captured you?" She shuddered. "Was it awful? Did they hurt you? Did they call you a dirty Jew?"

"A little slower, my dear little cat," his father said. "He's just home. Let him catch his breath."

"He's lost weight." His mother felt his arms. "Look at his face—the hollows. He lost his cheeks."

"Yes, Ma, that's what I said," Irv commented.

Jack leaned back against the couch and looked from one to the other of his family. There was gray in his mother's hair that he didn't remember. Marcia was taller, Irving was smoking a pipe. But his father was pacing the way he always had.

Jack didn't want to talk or move. If he could stay this way forever, he thought, he'd never want anything else.

That night he slept in his old room, the one he'd shared with Irv for years. Nothing had changed. Irv's bookcase and desk were still in the hall to leave room for Jack's folding cot. It was set up next to the radiator. When he sat down, he could reach out and touch Irv's bed. Irv's books were piled all over his bed.

"How's college?" Jack said.

"Good. I finished my second year. Dean's list."

Jack nodded. Irv was the smart one in the family. It was strange being in this room with him again. He wondered what his brother really thought of him. Did he resent Jack's having gone into the Army? The fuss that was being made over him now? With his rheumatic heart Irv could never have served, but he'd wanted to.

Irv relit his pipe. "So my little brother is a hero."

Jack grimaced. "No, it's not that way."

"What are you going to do now?" Irv said, drawing on the pipe. "You're going to be a year behind in school."

"I don't know if I'll go back."

"You can't go to college if you don't finish high school," Irv said.

Jack took off his clothes, folding his pants carefully along the seam, then folding them over the chair.

"You've gotten neat in your old age," Irv said.

"You learn that in the Army." Jack placed his shirt

over the pants. He found the cigarettes and offered one to his brother. Irv shook his head.

"How long have you been smoking?"

Jack took a deep drag. "A year. Since I went in."

"Ma's not going to like that."

"Everybody smokes."

"You know what you did was stupid, don't you?" Irv said.

"That isn't what I'd call it," Jack said, bristling.

"You never thought about the way Ma was going to feel! A whole year she didn't know anything, and then that missing-in-action telegram. That was a low blow. That could have killed her."

Jack stubbed out his cigarette. "I couldn't do things any other way."

"Then you shouldn't have done it!"

Jack kept grinding his cigarette out in the brass ashtray. Another remark from his brother and they'd be fighting, the way they used to.

"That note you left in the mailbox," Irv went on relentlessly, "those few words—Ma kept reading them over and over, trying to figure out where you were, if you were alive or dead. I told her you were all right. I thought of the Army, but I couldn't believe they'd take a fifteen-year-old kid."

"I didn't want to hurt Ma," Jack said. "I just had to get in. That's all I was thinking about. I didn't know they'd send an MIA telegram."

"Well, you're home now," Irv said. "What's done is done."

They finished getting ready for bed in silence. Irv shut off the light. Then out of the darkness he said, "I'm glad you're back, brother."

For a long time Jack didn't sleep. It was strange

being home, lying here in the same room with his brother. Strange and wonderful. He'd have to see Chuckie's parents soon, but not right away. And Dotty, he wanted to see her, too, but now that he was home he knew that neither visit was going to be easy.

For a few days Jack hung around the apartment, eating a lot and talking to his mother. He wanted to make up to her for all the months she'd worried about him. He wanted her to smile, to be happy. The way her face set sometimes when she thought she was alone hurt him. But when he talked to her, she brightened. She wanted to know everything he'd done, all the places he'd been. And over and over, she asked how in the world had he fooled them into letting him into the Army?

"I kept my mouth straight, I didn't smile, and I said 'sir' to everyone, the way Pop taught me."

His mother laughed. "So they thought you were a man." She pinched his cheek. "And I suppose you are. Jack, I admire your boldness. I was the same way. It runs in our family."

One afternoon Jack called Chuckie's parents from the phone downstairs in the hall. "Hello?" a woman said.

Jack cleared his throat. "Mrs. O'Brien?" Nervously he jingled the coins in his pocket.

"Speaking. Who is this, please?"

"Mrs. O'Brien, this is a friend of your son's, of Chuckie's. I was his best friend."

"Is this Jack?" she said. "Is this Charles's friend, Jack Raab?"

"Yes, Mrs. O'Brien, this is Jack Raab. Could I come see you?"

"Oh, I wish you would, Jack! You're home?"

"Yes, Mrs. O'Brien."

"Are you all right, Jack? Are you wounded?"

"I'm fine, Mrs. O'Brien." With all his heart he wished that he *could* tell her he was wounded. He felt that, somehow, that might ease the pain for her of seeing him alive and whole when her own son was gone forever.

"I'm so glad, Jack. Can you come over now? We want to see you. Mr. O'Brien and I want to see you, and so does Charles's younger brother. Charles wrote home about you all the time. Jack, he told us you had no mother, poor boy."

Deeply embarrassed, Jack stammered out that he would tell her all about it when he saw her. He walked through Bronx Park, up along the river, then back through Fordham University, and up Fordham Road where the O'Briens lived. It was a hot July afternoon. He thought about stopping for a beer, but he didn't want Mrs. O'Brien to smell liquor on his breath.

He was nervous about the visit, but he'd put it off long enough. He still had to see Dotty. He'd called and found out that she was away in Vermont, working at a summer camp. Her mother had given him the address. First he'd see the O'Briens, then he could think about Dotty.

Mrs. O'Brien met him at the door and embraced him. "Jack, come in, come in. You look just like your picture. You know Charles sent the picture of the two of you together." She drew him into the parlor. She was a short plump woman with the same red hair as Chuckie.

Chuckie's little brother, Danny, came into the room and stared at Jack. He was about ten years old, all

bones and elbows. "Hello, Danny." They shook hands.
Danny had red hair, too.

"You look just like Chuckie," Jack said.

"I know," Danny said. "I have his saxophone now."

"I didn't know he played sax."

Danny nodded. "In high school. It's mine now.
Want me to get it?"

"Sure," Jack said.

Mrs. O'Brien brought in cookies and tea on a tray.
There were starched white curtains at the window
and crocheted doilies on the couch, and pictures of
Chuckie in square gold frames crowded together on
a table.

"Is that Margie?" Jack said, picking up a picture
of Chuckie and a pretty dark-haired girl with their
arms around each other.

"Yes, that's our Margie."

"Chuckie talked about her all the time." Jack
started telling Mrs. O'Brien how he and Chuckie did
everything together. "Chuckie hated to get up in the
morning. I had to drag him out all the time."

Mrs. O'Brien laughed. "Charles always hated to get
up in the morning. Remember, Danny?"

In a little while Mr. O'Brien came home. "Give
Jack a beer. A soldier needs something more sub-
stantial than tea." Mr. O'Brien had a full head of
white hair and bright blue eyes. He didn't look at all
like Chuckie, but he was the same sort of outgoing
person.

Danny asked Jack about the war. "Did you get to
kill a lot of krauts?" He held the saxophone like a
machine gun. "Ak . . . ak . . . ak . . . ak. . . ." Then,
looking at the ribbons on Jack's chest, "You must
have killed a lot of them!"

Jack thought of the war stories he used to make up. Danny was that way now—fighting the Germans, winning the war singlehandedly, dreaming of being a hero.

"We dropped a lot of bombs," Jack said. "They did plenty of damage, but not just against war factories and bridges and things like that. A lot of those bombs fell on ordinary people."

"They were the enemy," Mr. O'Brien said.

"Yes, sir, they were."

"Why didn't my boy jump the way you did?" Mr. O'Brien said. "Why did he stay in the plane?"

Jack hesitated. It would have been nice to tell them that Chuckie died doing something heroic, maybe saving someone else's life. He could see on their faces that they were hungry for that kind of story.

"There was no way Chuckie could have bailed out," he said. "I'm sorry . . . but the minute the plane was hit, he was dead."

Mrs. O'Brien's eyes filled. She excused herself and left the room. Mr. O'Brien sat with his hands clasped, looking down. "So he died right away?"

"Yes, sir."

"Well, that's a mercy, anyway."

Mrs. O'Brien came back and sat down again. "Tell me about yourself, Jack. Is your father still in Alaska?"

Jack's face reddened. He put down his tea cup. "Well, Mrs. O'Brien, I have to tell you. . . . I have to say. . . . You see, I got into the Army with my brother's ID, and—"

"I didn't know you had a brother, Jack," Mr. O'Brien said.

"My mother, too," Jack said quickly. "I mean, she's living—"

"But, Charles said—" Mrs. O'Brien frowned. "Am I mixed up, Jack? I'm so sure he wrote that your mother —wait, let me get one of his letters—"

"No, Mrs. O'Brien, that's okay. Here's what happened." Jack told them the whole story. Danny listened, his eyes never leaving Jack's face, his mouth half open. It upset Jack. He could see that Danny was eating up the story. It was appealing to him as a great adventure, something he could dream about doing himself someday.

"My dear boy! I didn't know any of this."

"No, Mrs. O'Brien, I didn't tell Chuckie, I didn't tell anyone."

"So brave," Mrs. O'Brien said, patting Jack's knee. "Very brave!"

"No," Jack said uncomfortably, "I wasn't brave, Mrs. O'Brien, no braver than Chuckie. I was just lucky."

Later Mr. O'Brien walked to the bus stop with Jack. When the bus came, they shook hands, and Jack promised to visit again. "We want to see you," Mr. O'Brien said, patting Jack's hand. "We both want to see you again."

"I won't forget," Jack promised.

21

Jack stood on the highway, hitchhiking. He was on his way to Vermont to see Dotty. His uniform helped him get rides. He'd hardly put his thumb up when a couple in a thirty-seven LaSalle stopped for him and took him the rest of the way to the camp. It was beautiful country. Low mountains and green hills. From the road he could see a lake.

At the camp office he asked for Dotty. "Dotty Landon," a woman in shorts and a halter called over the PA system. "You're wanted at the office. Pronto!" The words rolled over the hills.

Jack saw Dotty coming up the hill and started down toward her. She was barefoot, wearing a green bathing suit. She looked up and he waved. Then they ran toward each other.

She was out of breath. His cheeks were burning. They embraced and kissed. His hand was on her bare back. She had her arm around his neck. It was wonderful! There was one kiss, then another. From above them on the hill a cheer arose. People had come out of the office and were watching.

"Very funny!" Dotty yelled up. She took Jack's hand, pulled him along with her to introduce him to everyone who worked in the office.

"So you did get here," the woman in shorts and halter said, smiling mischievously at Jack. "We wondered if you would."

"Be quiet, Lillian!" Dotty said, laughing.

She got permission to stay out till supper. A junior counselor would take over at the waterfront for her. "They're not overly strict here," she said. "Which is one of the reasons I like it." She led him down the hill. Jack followed her in a daze. He could hardly believe how beautiful and nice Dotty was.

She went flying down the path in her bare feet. He was having trouble. He felt clumsy and awkward. He was afraid that once she knew he was sixteen she wouldn't want anything to do with him.

"Dotty—" She was getting away from him. He stumbled in his heavy boots and went down, head over heels.

"Jack, are you all right?"

He let himself roll down the hill a few more times. It was just a relief to be silly and laugh.

They walked along a path skirting the lake. "I've got something to tell you," he said.

"I've got a million things to tell you. Jack, you're a hero." She looked at him. "I've told everyone how you bailed out of a plane, how you were a prisoner—"

He shook his head. He liked the way she was looking at him, but it was such a lie. Hero? Too much of a lie! "No. When I jumped out of that plane, I was just trying to stay alive. I was terrified."

"I would have been, too," she said.

"You know something I've been thinking about—all the time I was in, I never fired a shot at the enemy. I never did what I was trained to do."

"Why not?"

"Because war is crazy. People don't matter the way I thought. It's not men fighting each other. It's all machines and bombs and what your luck is. You just try to stay out of the way, just try not to get killed."

"I never thought of it that way."

"War is stupid."

"Yes, but, Jack—Hitler!"

"I know," he said. "I know we had to do it. I don't know if we could have done anything else. But almost anything has to be better than war, Dotty."

They sat down in a beached rowboat. He threw pebbles at the water. "I hope—" Jack cleared his throat. "I hope that what I'm going to tell you is not going to mean we can't be friends—"

"What is it?"

"It's nothing bad, I don't want you to think—"

"Is there somebody else, another girl?"

"No, it's nothing like that."

"Jack, were you wounded? Did something happen you didn't tell me about?" She sounded alarmed.

It was becoming so hard. "You're talking about something else," he said. "What I'm talking about is—" He scooped up a handful of pebbles. "—how old I am." He licked his lips. "Dotty, I'm sixteen."

"That's ridiculous," she said. "You're in the Air Force."

"No, I lied about my age." And again he explained.

"How extraordinary." Dotty looked at him. "You

did all that when you were only fifteen." Then she was silent.

Jack looked out at the water, squinting against the glare of the sun. He gathered little stones into a mound. She was searching for the polite way to tell him—*Go home, little boy.* So what was he sitting here for? *Get up, and go. Don't wait for her to tell you to go!* But still he sat.

Finally she nodded her head as if deciding something in her own mind. "I'm glad you told me, Jack. I can see why you didn't tell me sooner."

"I didn't tell anyone. I had to wait till the war was over."

"Yes, I can see that. Well. This is really something. I have to get used to the idea. I thought I could tell how old people were. I guess you don't act that young. Why should you, with all the experiences you've had. Jack, you're a very unusual person. I'm glad I know you."

There was a note in her voice that made Jack lift his head. "You don't mind?"

"Oh, maybe a little, in one way. No one likes to be fooled. But it would be awfully shallow of me to stop liking you because you're younger than I thought. I liked you before—why shouldn't I like you now?"

"I'm glad, but—" He didn't know how to say what was on his mind. He wanted to ask if she'd be his girl, but he didn't dare.

"We'll go on being friends," she said. "If that's okay with you."

"It's what I want," he said quickly. Then he blurted, "Will you go with me?"

"You mean steady?" She shook her head. "I

wouldn't, even if you were older, Jack. I'm serious about school, and I'm not going to get really involved with anyone yet." She squeezed his hand. "Don't worry, we'll still see each other."

They were both smiling, but he knew beyond a doubt that something *had* changed.

They went back to the camp. Dotty wanted him to meet her girls. The waterfront was full of little girls in rubber bathing caps. "Beaver Hut!" Dotty called, clapping her hands. A cluster of girls in orange and yellow bathing suits gathered around her.

"Girls, this is Jack Raab. He's just come back from the war."

"Hello!" the girls chorused. Jack smiled. All these eight- and ten-year-old girls looking at him!

"Are you Dotty's boyfriend?" one said.

"What's your name again?"

"Are you going to stay for a while?"

"What are you—a captain?"

"No, stupid. He's a sergeant."

Jack looked from one to the other, smiling.

"Why don't you talk?" one girl with braids said. She turned to Dotty. "Is something the matter with him, Dotty?"

"Talk," Dotty said to Jack.

"Hel-lo," he said, in a deep voice. The girls applauded.

"You're a hit!" Dotty said.

They spent the rest of the day together. Jack stayed overnight at a nearby boardinghouse and saw Dotty in the morning before hitching back to the city.

"Write me," Dotty said, standing with him at the entrance to the camp. "Okay, Jack? I'll write you back."

He wanted to kiss her, but it wasn't easy now. He touched her arm. She put her arms around his neck and kissed him.

For the rest of the summer Jack spent most of his time with other vets who were gradually returning to the neighborhood. They were all older than he was. Kids his own age didn't seem to know how to act with him. Even his old neighborhood friends acted embarrassed around him. He didn't feel as if he belonged anywhere. Even at home things had changed. The excitement over his return had passed, everyone was busy, and his parents wanted him to make up his mind about the future. It irritated his father that Jack was doing nothing, and his mother got upset at his smoking and drinking.

He woke up late every morning, dressed, and left the apartment. He hung around a pizza joint or upstairs in the Allerton Bowling Alley. Sometimes he'd meet another vet, and they'd talk about the Army, the war, what they had seen, what they had done.

All day Jack would talk, eat pizza, smoke, drink beer. Then when he came home his mother would smell the beer. There would be an argument. He didn't care that much about beer or even smoking. What he didn't like were the restrictions, explaining his comings and goings, having to apologize if he forgot himself and swore a little.

It was hot all through July and August. The war in Asia was dragging on. The newspapers were full of speculations about General MacArthur invading Japan. A lot of the vets Jack met were only home on furlough, but everyone expected the war in Asia to be over soon.

One weekend Jack took the train up to Buffalo to

see Stan. That broke up the monotony. Stan had had enough points to get out of the Army and was already working with his father as a plumber's apprentice.

Jack didn't know what he was going to do. He hadn't made up his mind about school, or work, or anything else. He kept putting it off. That's what he did best that summer—putting off things, drifting, not concentrating on anything. Now that he was out of the Army he had nothing to focus on, nothing to dream about. He didn't know what he wanted. It didn't matter that he said to himself, You're the only one who survived, so you have to make your life mean *something*. How else could he understand why he had lived, and they had died? But he had no idea what that *something* was.

Late in August the news came about the United States dropping the atomic bomb on Hiroshima, and after that on Nagasaki.

A few days later the Japanese surrendered. The war was over. Everyone poured out into the streets, screaming and dancing. Jack was out there, too, dancing in the streets.

The newspapers said the atomic bombs had saved a lot of American soldiers' lives by ending the war fast. It was true it had saved American lives, but the bombs had done it by killing civilians. Ninety thousand in Hiroshima, and forty thousand in Nagasaki. More kids and women killed than soldiers. It was a hard thing to understand. No easier to understand for Jack than the Germans' killing ten thousand Jews a day, day after day and week after week.

In September he went back to Christopher Columbus High School. Everybody wanted him to go back to school. His parents, Irv, and Dotty. "Sure, you're going back," Dotty said when they saw each other at the end of August. "What else, Jack? It's either that, or get a job. No, you'd be crazy not to at least get your high-school diploma."

Jack wasn't the only veteran returning to school, but he was the youngest. Getting used to school again wasn't easy. He had trouble concentrating, even sitting still was a problem. And although he was only a year behind his own class, he felt ten times older than everyone else.

Weekends he spent a lot of time at Dotty's house. They didn't do anything special. Half the time she had schoolwork and he'd just hang around, doing his own work, or listening to music. It was a long trip to Coney Island, two hours each way, but he didn't care. He could talk to Dotty better than he could to anyone else. It was too hard with his parents—they were always urging him to try harder, settle down, be like his brother. Dotty was easier, and what she said made sense to Jack.

"The first thing you do is stop worrying about your brother. Irv is Irv, and Jack is Jack. The next thing is finish high school."

"And then what?"

"And then you'll see. You don't have to figure your whole life out in a day. You've got plenty of time."

It was becoming clear that while they were going to remain friends, that's what they were—friends. More and more Dotty acted like an older sister to Jack—warm, interested, friendly, but definitely non-romantic. But, still, he liked being with her.

In November on Veterans Day the school had a special assembly honoring the students from Christopher Columbus who'd been in the service. All of them were asked to come dressed in their uniforms that day and to take a place of honor on the stage.

The principal, Mr. Wood, asked Jack, as the youngest veteran, to say a few words. "I'm not asking you to make a speech." Jack agreed, although he had no idea what he would say.

When his mother heard that he was going to speak, she said she was coming to the assembly. She called Mrs. O'Brien and invited her, too.

"Ma, for God's sake," Jack said. "I'll make a fool of myself."

"No, you won't. Just get up there and say what's in your heart."

On the day of the assembly Jack still didn't know what he would say, or how he'd have the nerve to say anything to a hall full of hundreds of people. It was strange going to school in his uniform. The kids in his class stared at him.

On the stage, along with the student veterans, about two dozen guys and four girls, were veterans from the First World War, the American Legion, the Jewish War Veterans, and the Veterans of Foreign Wars. The school band played the "Star Spangled Banner" as a color guard presented the American flag. Then a priest and a rabbi each said a prayer for the ones who had died.

The principal made a speech. "Today we are honoring the boys and girls from our high school who served our country. We won the war. Now we must win the peace. To win this peace each of you must get behind the peace effort the way you got behind the war effort."

The principal got a big hand. Then he introduced the representatives of the veterans' organizations, and the color guard. And last he introduced the student veterans.

As each name was called, and each one was asked to stand up, Jack grew increasingly nervous. It took Mr. Wood a long time to reach Jack's name. He introduced everyone else first.

When his name was finally called, Jack stood at attention. Mr. Wood told briefly how Jack had bailed out and been a POW. "But what I really want to emphasize is that Jack Raab might be the youngest soldier of World War Two. We're proud of Jack! His country is proud of him!"

The veterans on stage clapped. The kids cheered and whistled. It was real hero stuff. Jack stood at attention, his face getting hotter and hotter.

"Now I think Jack wants to share a few thoughts with us," Mr. Wood said, stepping aside for Jack.

Jack went to the podium. He looked out over the audience. He saw kids he knew. Everyone was watching. He saw his mother and Mrs. O'Brien sitting together.

"My name is Jack Raab," he started. His mouth was dry. "I was in the Eighth Air Force. I'm a Jew. I wanted to go and fight Hitler. I got in the Air Corps by lying about my real age." He stopped. The auditorium was dead still. He gripped the sides of the podium.

"Go on," the principal whispered.

"I'm glad I served." Jack licked his lips. He wanted to say something true and real that would reach all the kids out there listening and looking up at him. He didn't want them to look up at him that way, as if he had done something great.

"I'm glad we won," he said. "We couldn't let Hitler

keep going. We had to stop him. But most of all, I'm glad it's over." Had he said enough? There was a silence . . . a waiting silence. There was something more he had to say.

"I don't like war. I thought I'd like it before. But war is stupid. War is one stupid thing after another. I saw my best friend killed. His name was Chuckie O'Brien. My whole crew was killed." Now he was talking, it was coming out, all the things he'd thought about for so long. "A lot of people were killed. Millions of people. Ordinary people. Not only by Hitler. Not only on our side. War isn't like the movies. It's not fun and songs. It's not about heroes. It's about awful, sad things, like my friend Chuckie that I'm never going to see again." His voice faltered.

"I hope war never happens again," he said after a moment. "That's all I've got to say."

He sat down. He hardly heard the applause. The floor of the radio room was still slippery with Chuckie's blood. . . . Dave was still fumbling with his chute . . . the plane was still falling through the sky. . . .